C000117809

Charles Moberly

Tancava
P R E S S

Cooee Baby

by Charles Moberly

Copyright © 2024 Charles Moberly

Cover Design © 2024 Cathy Helms Avalon Graphics

ISBN

978-1-7398800-6-4 Paperback

978-1-7398800-7-1 e-book

Published by Tancava Press

https://charlesmoberlyauthor.blogspot.com/

PART I

My mother named me Awhina, cow that she is. You can't even shorten it. Aw? Hin? A hinny is a cross between a horse and a donkey. Ina? In a what? So, when I asked her why she'd chosen the name Awhina, she said it was Maori, and she liked it. What am I supposed to do? Like, dance the *haka* and stick my tongue out? So, I do, to her, to Professor Coulter, and my dad, but he's so dozy he doesn't notice. Dad runs an engineering company. He lives it. In his mind he never leaves it, which is dangerous when he's coming up to a road junction in his car. Does he know I exist? Hi there, Dad, I'm your daughter. No you're not, you're a widget. Can you increase the production of socket weld flanges? Thought not, you don't exist.

It's rare for my mother, the Tyrannosaurus, to justify anything, but she tried once. 'I gave you a

Maori name because you've got dark skin and a flat nose. You could pass as a Polynesian.'

True, my skin is dark, but flat nose? I spent the next eight years peering into the mirror, looking for a flat nose which wasn't there. So, I told her she was wrong.

'It was flat when we named you.'

'Like all tiny babies have flat noses, who look as though they should still be in an incubator.' I stormed out, kicking the door.

No one I meet knows how to pronounce the name Awhina, but those who claim they do say anything from a whiner (how charming), to a weaner (a piglet which has just been taken away from its mother, lucky little bastard), to Athena. So that's what I've become, a Greek Goddess to all but my mother, who calls me a weaner, and my father, who simply grunts, most appropriate.

Before I went to uni, I was having a sleepover at my friend Molly's house. My mother came to pick me up and phoned from outside.

'Are you ready, a weaner?'

'Coming'.

She barged into the hall, just at the moment when I was kissing Molly goodbye. All right, it was on the mouth, but since we'd spent the night together doing nothing worse than tickling each other's backs, it was, you might say, unfortunate that my mother saw us kissing.

She didn't say anything at first, but I did. 'Why didn't you ring the bell?'

'You said, "Come in".'

'No, I didn't, I said, "Coming".'

She shrugged, but when I'd buckled up my seatbelt, she turned on me.

'Now, look here, young lady, you need to sort yourself out. What you need – well, there are several things you need – but the most urgent is for you to meet some decent young men.'

Her words were not enough. She had to follow it up with deeds. 'I've invited Simon round to tea.'

To tea? What century are we living in? Is Simon going to be most impressed by my scintillating conversation, my boobs, or the way I crook my finger while sipping Darjeeling? If you're wondering whether I attended, I did. I put on my black and silver goth outfit, the one with all the chains, greased down my hair on one side, snatched at the sandwiches before Simon was offered one, chewed with my mouth open, and said virtually nothing the whole evening. But at least I saw off Simon.

'A weaner, you can't go through life behaving like that. When something interests you, you babble like a parrot, but if you don't like a situation, you're as mute as a statue. It's very rude.'

That was rich coming from someone who gobbles like a turkey.

....

Now I'm an undergraduate waiting for the results of my tripos exams at Cambridge University. It was a done deal that my A level results would be good enough to get me there, but how I survived the interview I will never know. The floor creaked as I walked across the ancient room. I was ready for the

3

farting chair or one where I would sink so low that they would be gazing down on me. But no, we sat around a table on equal terms. There were three of them. I wasn't going to be intimidated, so I gave each of them my hard stare. One of them couldn't take it and looked away. I made them laugh when I hadn't meant to. I described Professor Tully as blinkered and used the word 'crap' when asked my thoughts on the constraints of the speed of light. But when I talked about quantum mechanics, I knew my answers were better than their questions. I noticed one of the interviewers squirming in his seat, rubbing his hands, and grinning at his colleagues. One looked stony-faced, but the other nodded.

I don't have friends, apart from Lily, and she's only a sort of friend. I don't feel comfortable when I'm with people. I suppose I'm frightened they might expect some sort of relationship to develop. When I'm with my fellow students, I only relax if we're talking about academic subjects. Then I feel confident.

I got thrown out of Professor Coulter's lectures twice. The first time was when I said, 'He's talking utter bullshit,' too loudly. He was.

He was on the second occasion, too. He was banging on about all the wonderful advantages of attempting to contact intelligent life beyond the solar system. So I challenged him. 'If humanity does everything just because it's capable of doing it, then humanity will destroy itself.' I heard a few half-suppressed sniggers and rather more gasps.

Professor Coulter carefully adjusted his face in an attempt to look even more stuck-up than he already was. 'This is not a philosophy lecture. Can we return to the science.'

I wasn't having that. 'But you've propounded all the advantages of communicating with potential extra-terrestrial life. Are we not going to hear any of the disadvantages?'

'Ms Fernandez, will you please leave this room now. We can have a discussion in private on the science of disruption.'

That raised a few titters, but I think most of the students heard me mutter 'Prick' as I walked as slowly from the room as my anger would let me. And I hope everyone saw how I was holding my fingers behind my back. I'm cleverer than he is, and he knows it.

Professor Kovacs is very different. His white hair looks as though it's been shot through with static electricity. How his tiny spectacles stay on his nose, I will never know. He lets me scribble mathematical formulae across his whiteboard, which I can do three times faster than he can. He makes mistakes; I rarely do. He slaps his forehead with the flat of his hand. '*Hülye!*' Having deprecated himself in his thick Hungarian accent, he adds, 'Where would we be without you, Athena?'

Coulter had me up before the Discipline Committee for plagiarism, of all things, the tosspot. The result was that I bodied him. I'd been helping Zainab Nawaz, and dickhead decided that the contents of her essay were too close to mine. Right, so I decided to pretend that it was Zainab who'd helped me, rather than the other way round, just to confuse them. When the Investigating Officer

5

interviewed me, I secretly recorded our conversation. I was careful to use sufficient hints for him to draw the wrong conclusions, without incriminating me or Zainab. When we were hauled before the full Discipline Committee, I introduced so many contradictions that they became baffled. When the Investigating Officer claimed I'd said things which I hadn't, I played the recording from my phone and made him look an arsehole. But my real target was Coulter, so I gave him my best clapback.

'I believe Professor Coulter has become confused,' I said sweetly. 'But I think you should be lenient with him. He's brilliant in his field, but sometimes he struggles when presented with too many facts.' So Coulter, coward that he is, instead of trying to defeat me, which he had no chance of doing, turned on Zainab. I gave him my withering stare normally reserved for losers who think they can come on to me. 'Professor Coulter, since we've established that I helped Ms Nawaz with her essay but am not guilty of plagiarism, it cannot be possible that she is guilty either.' By that time the Chair of the Discipline Committee had heard enough. Both Zainab and I were acquitted. Coulter then tried to get me for making the recording and for insulting a professor. I pointed out that under the terms of reference of the Committee, a new charge could not be raised during the course of a hearing. Check mate.

If it wasn't for Coulter, I'd be totally confident of getting a first-class degree: Awhina Fernandez BA Hons (Cantab). That's if Coulter hasn't stuck his oar in.

My subject is astrophysics. That includes a lot of mathematics. On the side, I've submitted two papers to *A & A*, that's *Astronomy and Astrophysics* Magazine, one on Quantum Electrodynamics and the other on Quantum Vacuum. Both have been rejected. Just for the fun of it, I sent off a paper to *Mathematics Magazine* about the Hardy-Littlewood zeta-function conjectures. That got returned too. My problem is that I haven't got the qualifications or the reputation, yet.

As regards my degree course, I often go off-piste. A few of us scientists believe that it is dangerous and utterly stupid to attempt to make contact with intelligent life in the universe, and history shows us why. Stephen Hawking was one who thought it a bad idea. But still these knobs persist, because they can. It's mankind's greatest folly. And Coulter doesn't even want to talk about it.

I love it here in Cambridge. When I see the shadow of the central tower spread across the quad in the moonlight, I get goosebumps. The beautiful buildings, the knowledge that I'm following Isaac Newton, Charles Darwin, Francis Crick, and Stephen Hawking, that's humbling. But I'm not humble. I only have to appear at one of Professor Kovacs' lectures to know that my fellow students are in awe of me, as is the man himself.

I'm at the spearhead of scientific development. I may not have many friends here, hardly any in fact, but I'm brilliant at networking around the world, period. I'm confident online, but if I've got to meet anyone, I'm baby. I know I upset people. When they dis me, it doesn't bother me. The reason why I'm so respected in America is that I don't soften my views with typically British froth.

I'm applying for a PhD in astrophysics. Work on my research proposal has already begun. I'm more than confident that it'll be accepted. I've already got many ideas for my thesis, but I mustn't get ahead of myself.

....

Am I attractive? I don't know. People certainly give me lingering glances. When I was in my mid-teens, I thought everyone was throwing shade at me. I must look a freak, I told myself. I'd just wanted to look normal, to blend in with the crowd, to use a ghastly cliché. But more recently I've learnt to read people's faces a bit better. I can see it in their eyes when they look at me that they're admiring me and sometimes, shit-arses, lusting after me.

Up until a year ago, I'd tried not to think about my face and body. But then I decided to stop avoiding the subject and give myself a critical once-over. My eyes are a dark shade of mocha and so round that they've always embarrassed me. I couldn't get the word "moony" out of my head. My nose, for all the crap which T-Rex threw at me, is actually well-proportioned. My mouth is full and wide. I've always been so-o embarrassed by its width, thinking I must be a frog. My caramel-coloured skin seems to be smooth and unblemished, but with a tendency towards oiliness. I shine when I don't want to. My cheeks are on the full side, and perhaps everything about my face is too broad. My chin is... a chin. It seems to be the right size in the right place. As for my figure, it's so fucking normal that I must have been bought off a peg. I'm neither fat nor thin, tall nor short. I keep fit by running most days, and I have my bike to ride around Cambridge. Exercise helps me think better.

Do I care if I'm attractive? It pisses me off that actually I do, as you can tell from all this narcissistic self-analysis. The word "attractive" bothers me. Who do I want to attract? Not that creep Josh. He's so cringe. One eye follows my thighs and the other my tits, with his tongue hanging out metaphorically. At least he's so shy that he doesn't attempt to speak to me, which is more than can be said of Adam. I can't help looking at Adam when I don't want to. But when he approaches me, I freak out. I blush, I flush, in spite of my dark skin. I suffer from the vapours, and generally behave like a Victorian maiden, panicking because her chaperone is nowhere to be seen. I freeze. I must be frigid, but I know I'm not. When I'm near Adam, I'm warm, and he's hot. I mutter and stammer, until he asks me out, and then I simply say nothing.

Then there's Lily. I have the same feelings towards her as when I look at Adam. Lily does talk to me, and I feel warm, very warm, when I'm with her. Her movements are exquisite. She's studying law, so we can't talk shop, but we go for drinks together and laugh. She never mentions a boyfriend. I've never seen her with one. I don't go to parties; I'm too frightened to be left on my own with someone I don't know. That would freak me out and I'd refuse to speak. It's what I do when I feel awkward. So I stay in my room imagining Lily dancing. Lily disturbs me. I don't know what to do about her.

And now that creepy tool Josh has actually come on to me. I was sitting on a bank of the River Cam in the sunshine, thinking I might be near to cracking a particularly knotty formula, when I found him standing over me. Bitch no. I looked up past the pathetic fluff on his chin and gave him my long, cold stare. I'm rather proud of it. I tuck my chin in, lower my head, and freeze, like a cat ready to pounce, making sure that I don't blink. Josh didn't say anything, just stood there grinning, teeth to the fore. I snapped my notebook shut and stood up. He sort-of gulped, like a frog with indigestion.

'Can I sit with you for a while?'

'You can't, I'm standing up.'

He looked bumfuzzled. 'I've seen you so often. I'd like to get to know you.'

'Swerve.' He just stood there. What a loser. I realised that a well-aimed knee wouldn't just have the wet wipe doubling up in agony. If I gave him a good shove, I would be able to propel him backwards into the river. Instead, I decided to use my best put-down. 'You've only just met me, and already you're assuming I've got bad taste.' I'm probably not the first person to have said that, but I did think it up myself. Before he had time to respond, I'd walked away. I was pleased that I'd seen him off, but annoyed that I'd lost the thread of my formula, just as it was becoming clear.

And now I've had a drink with Adam. Lily had invited me to join her in the pub, and there they were, sitting on a padded bench in the lounge bar, grinning at me. I sat down on a hard chair opposite them. Adam went to buy me a drink, while I sat jerking my fingers towards Lily and hissing with a questioning look, trying to get her to explain. All she did was smile at me. After Adam had returned, I spent the next half-hour leaning across the table, attempting to see whether they were touching. They weren't. I wanted not to look at Adam, and when I did, he seemed to be asking me some sort of unspoken question. As for Lily, she just looked smug. I tried to think whether she was showing off that she'd made a sneaky link with him, or if she was merely pleased that she'd managed to bring us together. In which case, why didn't she leave us to it? I was thrashing about in my mind as to which of them I wanted to be alone with, and concluded Adam, Lily, and neither, which was no conclusion at all. Eventually I made a feeble excuse and left. A week later, nothing further has happened between me and either of them.

....

I bumped into Lily on St John's Street. Bitch no, she's only gone and done Botox. Her lower lip is so swollen that it hangs out, making her look like Tweety Bird with a permanent sulk. Her upper lip is so puffed out that it casts a shadow, making it look like she's got a moustache. Lily's face was so expressive before. It was lush, pliant, and kissable, not that I ever have. Now her mouth can only open and close, like a pouting goldfish.

'Fancy coming to the pub tonight?'

'Will Adam be there?'

'Do you want him to be there?' Before the Botox, she would have curled her lips into a teasing smile. Now all her face could do was look stuffed.

I didn't answer. When I got to the pub, Lily was alone. I couldn't help laughing at her.

She peered at me peevishly. It was the only way she could peer. 'Why are you laughing?'

'Nothing.'

'Come on, Athena, it must be something.'

'My lips are sealed.' I started choking at my own brilliance. I couldn't tell whether she saw the joke. She didn't smile, because she couldn't. Ten minutes later, I started laughing again. I was thinking of her kissing Adam, with him stuck onto those massive labia by suction. I imagined them going in an ambulance like that to hospital, and then a nurse inserting a pin, and a mass of gunky fluid shooting out, so that Adam could be released.

It wasn't a successful evening. Lily thinks she's bougie, but it was like having a conversation with someone's letterbox.

. . . .

The long vac is looming. It's only ten weeks away. Although I can work on my research proposal and my thesis, the prospect of spending three months being harangued by the Tyrannosaurus, ignored by Dad, and avoiding having tea with Simon, fills me with dread.

I'd gone home for a long weekend. T-Rex and I

were sitting in the conservatory, which smelt of geraniums and mould.

'How about a five-week cruise?'

'What? Who with?'

'Just the two of us. Your father won't come. Getting ten minutes off work is too much for him. But you could bring a friend. I'm sure your father would pay. Have you got any friends?'

The idea of being cooped up in a prison ship with my mother for five weeks was horrendous, and OMG, we would have to share a cabin.

'Where would the friend sleep?'

'Well, if it's a male friend, you would have to share a cabin with me. But if you brought a girlfriend, you could share with her. Take a look at this brochure. There's lots of exciting things for you to do, plenty of activities, sports, and there are frequent lectures on board to keep that funny brain of yours stimulated. Oh, and you can work on your thesises while you're at it.'

'They're theses, not thesises. And anyhow, I'm only working on one, so it's a thesis.'

'A weaner, you can be so pedantic.'

'It's not pedantic, it's precise. I'm a scientist. It's also called being correct.' I didn't know why she was being so salty. I got up to let a bumblebee out of the window.

The more I studied the brochure, the more my mood changed from scepticism to interest to something near enthusiasm. The boat was a small one, eighty-six passengers. That meant less chance of getting away from T-Rex. But I realised that it wouldn't be one of those cruises which docks for a single day in every port, just long enough to rush off on some tour, then spend a frantic hour checking the time in a café before dashing back to the ship, with two thousand people ruining the place they were meant to be enjoying. More often than not, this cruise would spend two or even three full days in each location. There were loads of sporting activities: snorkelling, horse riding, wind surfing, and much more. I wasn't particularly sporty, like competitive sporty, but I was quite spunky, and I liked trying new things. And some of the lectures did look intriguing.

So did the destinations. No standard trip from Miami to the Caribbean, this. It was in the Far East, around some of the most exciting islands I could think of: Bali, Sulawesi, Maluku Archipelago, and Papua New Guinea. I'd already passed from a state of being intrigued to being hooked. Except for one thing: sharing that cabin with T-Rex. I needed a companion, and she'd already said that Dad would pay for one. So, who could that be? I decided to pluck up courage and invite Lily and her lips.

'That's so sweet of you, Athena. I would love to come with you, I really would, but I'm going to be hiking in the Alps, followed by three weeks in Menorca.'

Who else? Molly and I had rather drifted apart since we'd gone to separate unis.

'How are you doing at Cambridge, Athena? I bet you're having a great time and have made lots of friends. A cruise? I'd love to, but I'm off to Australia for a large part of the vac.'

Zainab? No good asking her, her parents

wouldn't let her, nor her brothers. They wouldn't even allow her to play sports. Scuba diving in a hijab would be interesting. And I did swear too much.

No girlfriends, then. Boys? I didn't know any. Adam? Mmm, the idea was attractive. Attractive, I smiled to myself. But I could hardly ask him to spend five weeks on a ship with me when I'd only been out with him once, and that was when I'd sat there saying almost nothing, with Lily grinning smugly at me.

Stumped, unless... I could register with one of those dating agencies. "Desperate student seeks young man of similar age, to spend five weeks together cooped up on a ship being chaperoned by the applicant's mother." I might get further with a lesbian dating agency, but then a willingness to have sex would be implied. A female companion, with no suggestion of sex? There probably were such agencies, but what if we didn't get on, two incompatible spinsters snoring together in one cabin for five weeks? No thanks.

. . . .

When I was in my early teens, T-Rex hauled me before Dr Pelham.

'It's a behavioural thing, doctor.' She then spent the next five minutes listing all the things she thought were wrong with my personality, which seemed to be everything. When at last she'd shut up, Dr Pelham started asking me questions about what I liked and disliked. I was so angry that I refused to speak, so I just stared at him with my mouth closed.

He referred me to a psychiatric unit. T-Rex wasn't allowed to go with me, so I decided I would enjoy myself.

I was made to watch scenes of young people my age doing boring things. I was filmed watching them. Then some of the characters started looking into the camera, inviting me to take part. I thought they were fucking stupid. At the end, I was asked to give my impressions of what I'd seen in my own words, as if I was likely to use anyone else's. So, I poured forth a torrent of expletives which expressed exactly what I thought. The shrink tried to look professional, but her rapid blinking gave the game away. The language, memory, and cognitive tests were so easy that I doubt if I made a single mistake.

A fortnight later, T-Rex told me I'd been diagnosed with Asperger's Syndrome. She wouldn't let me see the letter, so I looked up the symptoms myself.

Problems with social interaction. Tick.

Difficulty making and maintaining friendships. Tick.

Obsession with a narrow range of subjects. What's wrong with that? My thoughts are dominated by my fascination with astrophysics and mathematics. Is being an expert a crime?

Tendency to speak loudly. Tick.

Clumsy, unfortunately yes. Tick.

Heightened sense of fairness and honesty. Tick. I do have a sense of injustice, which is why I come up against that fraudster, Coulter.

Ability to concentrate. Tick. That's a virtue.

Ability to memorise detail, ditto. Tick.

Verbalising thoughts which most people keep private. Yeah, I do say what I think.

Difficulty maintaining eye contact, absolutely not. I go the other way. I stare at people.

Treating information received as literal. Mmm, that's an interesting one. I say what I think, so I expect others to do the same. I don't expect people to speak in niceties. If they do, I ignore the waffle and assume the literal. So, tick.

After all this, I was sent on a weekly course of Cognitive Behaviour Therapy. Although I skipped a few of the sessions because I was busy, I did enough to conclude that it was a fucking waste of time.

....

I don't go to Formal Dinners in Medieval Hall, because I don't associate with members of my own college. In fact, I don't go there for meals at all, formal or informal. I prefer sandwiches or takeaways in my room. When Lily invited me as a guest to a Formal Dinner at her own college, I told her no way. But then she dangled an enticement in front of me.

'I can arrange for Teddy Bleasdale to join us.'

In case you're wondering, Teddy wasn't a turn-on, absolutely not. But he was in the same year as me, reading astrophysics. We did share many of the same progressive thoughts, and like me he thought Professor Coulter was an arsehole.

'You clever little cow,' I said to Lily. 'All right, I'll come, provided we can talk dark energy.'

She would have screwed up her face in mockery, had not the Botox frozen it.

Her Dining Hall was rather special. Candlelight flickered, white-gloved waiters and waitresses served a delicious meal with rather good wine, and I couldn't help being impressed by the portraits of some famous college alumni hanging on the panelled walls.

I nearly got thrown out when I first arrived. All right, I should have realised that formal dining required formal dress, but I had assumed that traditional surroundings didn't prevent us from living in the twenty-first century. How was I to know that catsuits were *verboten*? I thought I looked glam, and I could tell from some of the looks I got from other students, male and female, that I was right. Luckily, Teddy's pa is a Fellow, so I got away with a 'We'll let you in this time'.

I know the drink got the better of me, because when Teddy invited me to partner him to their May Ball, I first of all choked, and then actually said yes. What the fuck was I thinking? Lily says she's going with Adam and we can make a foursome. Why can't I stop thinking about four-poster beds? I wouldn't know which way to turn.

Lily was being all schoolmarmish. 'I think I'd better help you choose your outfit this time.'

'Right, Lily. Right. I get it.'

....

Tripos final results are out. I've got a First, as I knew I would. So, Professor Slimeface, you couldn't stop me, though I'll bet you tried. Ms Awhina Fernandez, BA Hons First Class (Cantab). Teddy got a 2.1. He seems pleased with it. Adam and Lily have another year to go. For me, it's onward with my research proposal, and when I've been accepted, I'll be on my way to becoming Doctor Fernandez.

. . . .

When I looked in the mirror, I kept asking myself whether the woman staring back at me was really Athena. I felt like a movie star. With goosebumps. My hair was bunched up in a way that managed to look both stylish and wild. Lily had persuaded me to go for satin, and together we chose ice blue as the colour. The gown was open at the back, loose and elegantly pleated at different angles across the bust, pinched in at the waist, and tight over the hips and bum. It clung to my left thigh, but on the other side an outrageous slit ran down from my hip to my ankle. I found that when I bent my right knee, I revealed the full glory of my unclothed leg. I giggled at Lily and did it again. She nodded approvingly and we high-fived. She herself was all in lemon, and I was as turned on by her as I was by myself.

Did I enjoy the May Ball? It's not easy for me to answer that. I see it all as a dream glimpsed through shifting mist. I suppose it was sort of romantic. We were the talented, the beautiful people, all four of us swinging through the college gates, arm in arm, knowing we looked good.

Electric string quartet. Were the musicians really dancing? Sparklers, champagne, canapes.

Everything free. Flinging my wheel hard over, driving my little car into Lily and Adam's, bang. Whoops. Teddy explaining the meaning of the word "dodgem". Cringe. Green and yellow lasers playing on the college walls. Thundering beat of Wedman Fuller. Lily and Adam dancing. Me, tottering in front of Teddy. Deciding I ought to get into the zone. Bumping into Professor Kovacs. No, I mean, really bumping into him. Nearly knocking the little man over.

'Is no problem, no problem. Oh, Athena, it is you. No problem.'

Explosion of fireworks at midnight echoing around Cambridge. Hundreds of pink and blue balloons meandering into the night sky, everyone cheering. Mobile steel band leading us through the streets. Chilling out in a marquee, having to share a beanbag with Teddy. Shoulders touching, not liking it. Standing up to get away from him. Looking towards Lily and Adam. 'How about another dance?' Lily pouting, 'Which one of us are you asking?' Music getting slower and slower. Being smooched by Teddy. Not comfortable, flesh tightening. Wishing it would all end.

It did end. Punt on the river at dawn, booked by Adam. Steam rising off the water, fucking cold. Snuggling under a rug with Lily. Another punt crashing into us, forcing us into the bank. Nose wedged into a sluice gate. Pressing my foot against an upright and giving a good shove. Big splash. Adam losing his balance and plopping into the teeth-chattering water. Whoops. Time for bed.

A few days later, I was sitting in a café enjoying the aroma of other people's coffee and the anticipation of mine sliding down the sides of my tongue. I'd just started to write a message to one of my online mates in California, when in walked Teddy. I tried to duck behind my screen, but he'd spotted me. I panicked, thinking the May Ball might have been an excuse for him to come on to me. I needed to divert him.

'Have you read my theoretical paper on Degradation of Serially Connecting Loops yet?

Teddy looked sheepish. 'Ye-es?'

'And?'

He sat down opposite me. 'Athena, it's seriously wacky.'

'Like, what does that mean?'

'It's unproven.'

'Of course it's fucking unproven, it's a theory.'

He looked embarrassed. 'Have you sent it to *A & A*?'

'Yep, and they rejected it. I've sent it to the *Astrophysical Journal* in the States. I've yet to hear from them, but in the meantime, I'd like to know what *you* think, if it's not too much effort.'

'So, it's extending Quantum Mechanics into an area where it's never been used before.'

'Right, so it is. Did you, like, find any errors in my formulae?'

'No, but look, Athena, it's a bit over my head. You're utterly brilliant and you'll go far. It's just that I can't keep up with you.'

'Have a good vac, Teddy.' I snapped my laptop shut, stood up, and walked off, leaving my coffee undrunk. I hadn't wanted him to think there'd be any follow-up to what might have happened at the May Ball. Talking about my theory was just an excuse to shake him off.

PART II

Awhina and her mother Diane flew to Bali and spent four nights there. They visited Tirta Empul temple and went up Mount Batur volcano to see the sunrise. Awhina loved the snorkelling and was thrilled to learn that there would be many more opportunities on the trip.

She and Diane went horse riding along a beach. Awhina found slosh-trotting through the surf boring after a while, so she turned her horse onto firm sand, clamped her heels into its flanks, leant forward, and flew along for over a mile at a fast gallop, laughing into the wind with the thrill of it. She liked the look of a green valley with terraced cultivation leading towards some hills to her left. She rode into it but was hurled into a rice paddy when her horse shied, slipped, demolished a bank made of mud, and then bolted, after catapulting her into stagnant water. She hauled herself out draped in vegetation, dripping with sludge, and spitting out dirty water. It took their guide nearly two hours to find her.

They were sitting at a restaurant overlooking the beach. The sun was about to set and some crab-eating macaques were squabbling on the sand in front of them.

'A weaner, I thought we had an agreement: I wouldn't nag you, so long as you behaved yourself.'

'My horse had a mind of its own.'

'No, it didn't. I've ridden horses all my life, and I could see what you did. You could have been hurt, the horse could have been injured, and I've had to pay out a fortune to the riding company, including compensation to the farmer for his damaged bank and rice crop, and to another man for a prize fighting cock killed by your bolting horse.'

Awhina gazed out over the surf, trying to shut her out. 'I'd like to have a diving lesson tomorrow. Diving's mentioned several times in the brochure, and I need to learn before we get to the best spots.'

'No, a weaner. Diving involves doing what you're told, something you never do. You can't take off by yourself like you did today, or you'll kill yourself. And sit up straight.'

Awhina booked herself into the diving lesson. She enjoyed it and did what she was told.

....

They boarded in the rain and sailed overnight on a tranquil sea to Sulawesi. Awhina loved the way the old ship creaked and pitched, even on the slightest of swells. She got up early the next morning and went up onto the sundeck before breakfast, rejoicing in the light flashing on the pristine water. She loved the white of the ship's wake stretching towards the horizon, and the way the humid air on her cheeks was cooled by the breeze as the ship rumbled through the tropic air. As she walked aft, even the fumes from the funnel seemed an appropriate part of the scene. Best of all, no one else was up, so she had these wonders all to herself. She felt alive, fresh, and eager with anticipation.

She went snorkelling with her mother, and the next day trekked to meet the Toraja people, with their *tongkonan* houses, shaped like massive ships, made of wood and thatch. They learnt about the tribe's elaborate death rituals. Awhina asked if she could see one. Her mother hissed at her to be quiet, and the guide ignored her.

Awhina sat on her balcony for most of the next day, working on her research proposal. It now contained more than just a structure; it had detail. She would need to discipline herself to keep it within the prescribed eighty thousand words. She couldn't resist planning her thesis at the same time. That was highly premature, because it was dependent on her proposal being accepted. But her mind was racing.

That night, there was a lecture on board, given by a pleasant woman called Penelope. The subject was *Remote Tribes of Indonesia*. Diane and Awhina were delighted to learn that there were over three hundred ethnic groups, and seven hundred languages.

Awhina turned to her mother. 'The most

interesting tribes are in Papua. It's the most culturally diverse place on earth. Many of them are still living in the stone age and are hunter gatherers.'

'Sush! Penelope's trying to talk.'

Penelope smiled good-naturedly at Awhina until she'd finished speaking.

Next day, they visited a waterfall. The pool was deliciously cool after the heat and humidity of the air. Awhina found that if she swam hard up to the fall, she could brace herself against two ledges and receive the full force of a power shower. When she let go, she was swept into the centre of the pool, where blue and orange butterflies fluttered around her head.

In the afternoon, she had a windsurfing lesson. It wasn't much good because there was little wind. She wobbled upright, stood for a minute or two, then was told that the direction of the breeze had changed, and that she should be on the other side of the sail. While trying to adjust her position, she invariably fell in. She drank a little seawater each time, and after a while felt queasy.

Two nights later, they sailed from Sulawesi in a brilliant sunset. It was around this time that Awhina noticed a man looking at her frequently and smiling. She wished he wouldn't. He was much older than her, probably around forty. He sat with a companion who leered at her in a way that made her even more uncomfortable. She'd heard them talking. They seemed to have Australian accents or something similar. She thought the first one was rather good looking and seemed confident, but she was careful not to be seen staring at him or returning his smile.

'Hi, I'm David.' Awhina nearly jumped off her barstool. Panicking, she almost wished her mother was with her. He seemed friendly and a bit intriguing. She did something which she rarely did with a man unless she had to: she smiled, a little.

'My friend Bruce has a touch of the skits, spending his evening in the dunny, so I thought I'd take this opportunity to introduce myself. I'm sorry I haven't done so before, but we seem to have gone on different excursions so far.'

'And my mother's nattering with a friend and will be at it for hours, knowing her.' She realised that her answer indicated that she was alone and available, whatever that meant. Had she been mildly flirtatious? She strongly hoped not.

'So, here we are. Can I buy you a drink?'

She sipped her Campari and ginger ale, sometimes looking at him and sometimes not. She noted his smell, pleasant, and his smile, comforting.

'So, do you have a name?'

'It's Athena.'

'A goddess, eh? Most appropriate.'

She wasn't going to explain the complications of her real name after that.

'So, what are you doing with yourself, and why this cruise?'

She briefly told him that she was at Cambridge University, and that she'd just graduated. She avoided any further details. As for the cruise, she told him how she was excited to be visiting such a remote and intriguing part of the world, how she'd enjoyed the horse riding, the trips, and the snorkelling, and how she was looking forward to doing some more diving after her first lesson. She explained her failure to learn to wind surf.

'I can solve that one. I do it all the time back home. I can teach you. It seems daunting when you start out, but once you're off, you'll never look back.'

'I was off rather too many times a couple of days ago.' OMG, she thought to herself, I've cracked a joke. What is this man doing to me?

They had another drink, and she opened up a little more. She told him she was looking forward to a lecture on board next week, entitled *Opportunities Offered by Technology*.

The T-Rex appeared. David was charming to her. Awhina couldn't read what her mother was thinking. Too old for me, I expect, she thought miserably.

They went to their separate tables at dinner. Now and then, David caught her eye and grinned. When she thought her mother wasn't looking, she glanced back without smiling. She felt ever so slightly fluttery. It didn't occur to her that she'd never asked him anything about himself.

....

The next night, they were sitting at the bar again. The ceiling was creaking as the ship pitched in a heaving swell.

'Bruce has come off the wiz box, but I told him I wanted to have a drink with you, and he took the hint.'

'My mother's got the squitters too, so she's staying in the cabin.' Already finishing her second

28

gin and tonic, Awhina was feeling light-headed. She giggled. 'Perhaps she caught it off Bruce.'

David pretended to look shocked. 'I'm glad you said that and not me.'

Awhina picked up a peanut, lobbed it towards her mouth, and missed.

'Look, why don't you join Bruce and me for dinner? We can't have you dining alone.'

The dinner was less remarkable than what happened after. Tactfully, David only encouraged her to have one smallish glass of wine. She pointed out that there was an opportunity to go wind surfing in two days' time. David said he would teach her, as she hoped he would. They discussed music and films, and Bruce talked annoyingly about himself. Still Awhina didn't ask anything about David.

They walked along the beach in starlight so strong that grains of sand glistened like silver crystals. After a while, David took her gently by the hand. He stopped walking and nestled against her before she could prevent it. Then came the kiss. The sweetness surprised her. She felt his hand move behind her waist and then pull her arching back towards him. They parted briefly, then joined again. She felt his tongue move ever so slightly against hers and was too startled to resist.

After a while, he broke off and patted her gently on the bottom. 'Mmm, you do that well.'

Do I, she wondered. She'd never done it before, although she didn't tell him that. A threshold had been crossed, carrying her into an experience which was instinctive, primeval, alarming. How many times had she heard people in movies, in books, in real life, say, 'I've just been waiting for the right man to come along.' And now, she wondered, perhaps he has.

....

Awhina got up early in the hope of seeing the sunrise before their arrival at Maluku. The sight which greeted her as she stepped on deck made her gasp. The ship was gliding past jungle-clad cliffs only a few hundred metres to her left. Cone-shaped islands were appearing ahead, mist clinging to their lower slopes. They rounded a headland and Awhina didn't know which way to look. Rows of thatched cabins on stilts clung to the water's edge. Aromas of sautéed garlic, mixed with moulding vegetation and drying fish, were drifting over the water and confusing her nostrils. She felt hungry but didn't want to return below deck. Across the bay, a formidable volcano was rearing upwards towards the sky. This was a paradise to eclipse Bali and Sulawesi. She was leaning on a rail, feeling the balmy air cancelling out the breeze from the motion of the ship. One smallish island had a dirty-looking fumarole at its summit, above which a wisp of sulphurous smoke was hanging. She wondered what would happen if it blew its top now. She'd secretly been hoping for a volcano to erupt or, better still, to experience an earthquake. It took an effort to leave the deck and join her mother for breakfast.

'You'd better put on your best frock this evening. We've been invited to dine at the Captain's Table. It's a great honour.'

'No, it isn't. Everyone gets invited in the end.'

'A weaner, stop it. And do try to behave tonight, just for once. I suggest you only speak when someone addresses you.'

Awhina took a shine to Captain Hasegawa. He had a calm and gracious smile, bowing ever so slightly before speaking to each of his guests in turn. Which meant mostly to answer Awhina's questions. Her natural curiosity ran away with her. She quizzed him relentlessly, often just as he was putting food into his mouth, which made it difficult for him to eat.

'Do you steer the ship yourself?'

'I sometimes take a turn, to keep my hand in.'

'How long are you away from home?' Captain Hasegawa dabbed at the corners of his mouth with his napkin. He'd only just taken a bite of lobster and was still chewing.

'Are you married?'

Was the first sign of irritation starting to spoil his smile? 'Yes, I am married.'

'Do you miss your wife?' Diane turned to look daggers at Awhina. An elderly lady coughed, possibly to show her disapproval, but unfortunately for her, it produced a fit of choking so violent that her husband had to thump her on the back. That saved Captain Hasegawa. He was able to express such concern for the poor lady that it was reasonable for him to avoid answering Awhina's latest question.

A short kicking match took place between Awhina and her mother under the table. Diane should have known better. It was bound to surface.

'If my mother would stop kicking me, I'd like to continue with our conversation. Captain Hasegawa, do you think this ship can sink?'

'Right, that's it. I'm sorry that my daughter is being so obnoxious, Captain. Thank you for a lovely meal. I'm only sorry that we have been forced to leave.'

Captain Hasegawa stood up, bowed, and smiled. With the departure of the spluttering lady and her husband, and now this peculiar and tactless young woman and her mother, the number of guests at his table had just halved.

....

The wind surfing lesson left Awhina breathless. It was partly the exhilaration, because long before the end she discovered she could actually do it. She progressed so well that she took off, zipping across the bay at high speed, tugging at the boom and playing with the wind. Since David hadn't yet told her how to turn round, they had to send a speedboat to bring her back.

She was also breathless because of physical contact with David. He looked good in his green and brown trunks, with his tanned and muscled body. He smelt nice. But it was the way he laid his hand so firmly between her shoulder blades to support her, and the way his instructions were commanding yet sympathetic, that made her so want to please him. And she knew that she did. She was a submissive yet determined pupil, and the triumph she felt when she first leant back against the wind and took off, managing to turn her head back towards him and grin, added to her sense of achievement and pleasure with herself.

She liked the way he let her carry her own gear back to the shack, then guided her firmly but gently to the beachside bar. He ordered a mojito for her and a beer for himself. They sat gazing at each other, smiling. She felt secure.

'You say you've graduated from Cambridge University. What next?'

She checked to see that he looked sincere and decided that he did. 'I'm going to take a PhD in astrophysics. I'm studying several things at once, some mathematical and some astronomical. I'm working on the Hardy-Littlewood zeta-function conjectures. I've made an important breakthrough. I'm going to show that Fenstein got it wrong. I'll tell you why.' She paused to sip her mojito.

He laughed. 'I think I'd better try one of the other ones.'

She looked shocked. He was grinning at her. 'Your other projects?'

She readjusted her thoughts, wondering why he'd said that. She decided he might be ready to receive her most treasured theory. 'Most scientists will tell you that so-called intelligent life cannot get to us, because the distances are too vast, and nothing can travel faster than the speed of light. Some of us believe that's naïve. Stephen Hawking said, "If aliens visit us, the outcome would be much as when Columbus landed in America, which didn't turn out well for the Native Americans. We only have to look at ourselves to see how intelligent life might develop into something we wouldn't want to meet." For the past few decades, humanity has been trying to broadcast itself from earth, hoping to make contact with life beyond our solar system. Some of it happened automatically, all that junk we transmitted from the time we first discovered radio. Then we started asking questions, deliberately trying to make contact.'

'Questions?'

'Sending signals which extra-terrestrials would be able to identify as intelligent, like who we were and where we resided. As you know, radio waves travel at the speed of light.'

'Of course I do.' He winked at her.

'So, what most scientists will tell you is that there is no chance of extra-terrestrial life getting to us, because the distances are just too great. Actually, far too many of them just don't care, because if there's an opportunity to attempt something new, they can't resist doing it.'

A flock of small birds came skimming across the surface of the water. Awhina took another sip. 'How old is the universe?'

'Strewth, I don't know. Many millions. Billions?'

'Thirteen point eight. How long have we had an advanced civilisation which can do things like fly and send radio messages? Would you say less than two hundred years?'

'I'd go for that.'

'The point is this: when we think of intelligent life, we imagine beings who, although they may look different to us, have roughly the same intelligence, or perhaps a bit more. But think of

34

those billions of years. Don't you see? They could have passed our state of intelligence millions of years ago?'

'So?'

'So here we are, sitting smugly on our planet, saying nothing can go faster than the speed of light, therefore there's no danger of intelligent life out there getting to us. Think back those two hundred years. Do you think the people then could have imagined what we know today? They were constrained by a limited view of the world. So are we. If you'd asked them how long it would take to get from the UK to Australia, they would have said about four months, because that's how long it took by boat. They couldn't have imagined that two hundred years later we'd be getting there in less than twenty-four hours, because they couldn't have imagined airplanes. Nor could they imagine instantaneous video calls across the world, because nothing created by man was capable of travelling faster than a steam engine. So to say that no one could travel faster than the speed of light is simply naïve, and dangerous. We've advanced two hundred years with our knowledge. Other civilisations could be thousands or millions of years ahead of us.'

David spread his hands. 'So, what's the problem? If these little spacemen are a million years more advanced than us, that'd be cool.'

'The chances are very high that it wouldn't be. All we have to go on is our own history. Give me one example of a so-called inferior civilisation which has benefitted from the arrival of a so-called superior one, and I'll give you twenty where the encounter has been disastrous. It's a basic law of evolution. The fittest survive and thrive because of their competitive advantage. It's called exploitation. That's before we get to the risk of new diseases.

'Still not convinced? Here's an analogy, if that helps. Three hundred years ago, a primitive tribe lived on a remote island, just like this one we're on now. For the first time, they saw a ship sail by. They'd never seen anything like it before. Some of them were worried. But others said, "no problem, look, their spears are blunt." The spears were guns. They hadn't experienced them, so they couldn't imagine them. Now don't you see?'

'Sort of.'

A middle-aged couple from the cruise ship who'd been sitting at the table next to them got up and left. The man shook his head sympathetically at David. Awhina had been talking loudly.

'Do you want me to explain the technicalities?'

'Er, I think we'll leave that one for now. So this is going to be your thesis?'

'It may form part of it. I've been up against a professor who's suffering from myopia. He doesn't understand how there could be any scientific advance which could possibly be dangerous to attempt. There's just one comfort in all of this. Civilisations and species get to the stage where they destroy themselves. That explains why there may not be many out there who've survived.'

'Some comfort.'

'It's called the Fernandez Curve.'

'Isn't your name Fernandez? Don't tell me...'

'I invented it. It goes like this. People live longer

and gain more comfortable lives. Civilisations grow until they become top-heavy. What had been sophisticated now becomes cumbersome and complicated. Longevity, which had previously been seen as advantageous, is now a burden. Technology is out of control, outstripping the ability of society to absorb it. Existential challenges require global co-operation, but humanity is rooted in confrontational mindsets which are hopelessly out-of-date. My professor actually believes in the Drake Equation and all its variants. Can you believe that?'

'I could if I knew what it was.'

'It's a gooky theory which guesses the likelihood of life in our solar system, while pretending to be scientific about it. It's pure speculation based on erroneous data. Every now and then some idiot sticks their finger in the air and changes it.'

David sat back and drained his beer. 'You really are something. Fancy another swim before dinner? I'll settle up for these drinks, and then I'll race you. First to get changed and into the water buys the first round in the bar. Is that a deal? Stay here and we'll start the race when I get back.'

She waited until he was at the bar, then slid out of her seat. She ran towards the ship, pleased with herself that she'd cheated.

....

'Who's that man I keep seeing you with?'

She was having breakfast with her mother on their balcony. There'd been a storm in the night, and the ship was ever-so-gently rolling, even though they were moored within the harbour. But the sun was trying to break through.

'His name is David. His friend is called Bruce.'

'And?'

'And what?'

'What else do you know about him?'

'Nothing, I haven't asked.'

'You mean you're seeing him, and you don't know anything about him?'

'I'm seeing that frigatebird over there, but I haven't asked it to explain itself.'

'Stop trying to be clever, a weaner. He's almost twice your age.'

'I mean, why are you so inquisitive? He's just a friend. You have friends. Do you put them through the Inquisition every time you meet a new one?'

'That's not the point.'

'What is the point? Age is so important in friendship, says no one ever.'

Afterwards, she realised that perhaps she should find out a bit more about David. What if he was married or already had a Sheila back home? So what? She was enjoying his company.

Later that day, Diane fell ill. It was diarrhoea again, but this time with vomiting. The ship's doctor asked to see Awhina.

'There's nothing for you to worry about, but I think we need to get your mother checked out at a hospital. I'm arranging for a helicopter to fly her to Bahtera on Sulawesi. If she doesn't improve, they can fly her from there to Jakarta, but it's most unlikely that will be necessary.'

'Should I go with her?'

'She'll be in good hands. There won't be anything you can do. It's best if you stay here. You can go in to her now.'

'Darling, I'm so sorry about this. I'll be all right. You stay here and enjoy the cruise. I'll be well looked after.'

Awhina nodded, then dashed forward and kissed her quickly on the forehead. She turned towards the door with the slightest prickle of tears forming in her eyes.

'Oh, and a weaner. Do look after yourself and be sensible.'

It didn't take her long to realise she would be alone in her cabin. She wondered what that would mean for her relationship with David.

. . . .

Over half the passengers had crowded into the main lounge where the furniture had been rearranged theatre-style. A few people were having to stand. Dr Oliver Belstead, the young man giving the lecture, surveyed his audience. A broad tongue of sandy-coloured hair flopped down over his boyish features.

'The subject of tonight's talk is *Opportunities Offered by Technology*. I want this to be as interactive as possible. Don't hesitate to stop me and ask questions at any stage, especially if you don't understand anything. Please give your name when you speak.'

Awhina thought he sounded enthusiastic but too eager to please.

'Right, let's get stuck in. My first topic is global warming. We know the dangers, we know that some of the problems are already with us, and we know that unless we do something about it urgently, those problems are going to get much worse.' He went on to describe various types of renewables: wind, wave, tidal, biomass, solar, and geothermal, before moving on to electrical and hydrogen powered vehicles. 'But the real Holy Grail is nuclear fusion. It's cheap, it uses a material which is readily available, and above all it's clean, with virtually no harmful emissions.'

'It's thirty to forty years away from being viable and productive.'

Dr Belstead committed his first mistake. Awhina had made a statement, not asked a question, and she hadn't given her name. He should have imposed discipline from the start, but he didn't.

'It may be, but we've already had a major breakthrough. For the first time, we've managed to create more energy than was input for the experiment.'

'That was minuscule. It will take decades for it to be scaled up to productive levels. By then it will be too late.'

Dr Belstead smiled indulgently at Awhina. If he wanted to move on, he was too slow.

She was already on her feet. 'We're not facing climate problems. We're facing a catastrophe. It will lead to deaths from so-called natural disasters: excessive heat, wildfires, flooding, and landslides. More and more of the earth will be uninhabitable, which will lead to famine, mass migration, conflict, and wars. The problem won't be tackled, because developing countries will always prioritise their own paths to prosperity in the short-term. We can see that in India and China today. It will be Africa next. And rich countries won't give up their extravagant lifestyles.'

'Your name is?'

'Athena Fernandez. I have a First Class Degree in astrophysics at Cambridge University.'

'Thank you for your input, Athena. That's very interesting.'

Awhina remained on her feet. 'There's a free-for-all going on in the Arctic to mine minerals and open it up for shipping. On land, Arctic permafrost has captured a trillion and a half metric tonnes of carbon over millennia. When that melts, microbes will release vast new amounts of methane and CO_2, as well as diseases from which we no longer have immunity.'

Dr Belstead hastily continued before Awhina could draw breath. 'I now want to move on to quantum computing.' Awhina was all for that. She supported Dr Belstead, adding to his enthusiasm, although she did get a bit too technical for the audience. Two women stood up and left, one staring at the floor, the other at Awhina, who'd sat down.

'My next topics overlap, so I'm going to take them together: robotics, artificial intelligence, and brain-computer interfaces.' Dr Belstead described each in turn, ending with, 'I'm really excited by this.'

Awhina was on her feet again. 'You shouldn't be, you should be terrified. These technologies are already outstripping society's ability to adapt to them socially and politically, and the gulf is getting wider exponentially. We're rapidly transitioning from not being able to adapt to not being able to control.'

'Too right, mate,' shouted Bruce.

A middle-aged man wearing a green shirt and a cravat stood up, turned towards Awhina, and said sourly, 'Roger Turner. Aren't we meant to be talking about opportunities here?'

She ignored him, but David didn't. 'David Grant. My understanding from Dr Belstead's opening remarks is that this is meant to be interactive. This lady here has put forward some counterarguments which I personally find interesting and relevant.'

'Thank you for your useful inputs,' Dr Belstead said quickly. He took a flustered drink of water.

The brief silence gave Awhina another opportunity. 'We cannot afford to pursue every new development just because we can. That is a path to self-destruction. If we don't control artificial intelligence, it will enslave us. There has to be some control. But that will only come if society is turned on its head. For now, our future rests in the hands of old and wealthy people who will not be alive to suffer the consequences. In the USA, the cult of the rights of the individual reigns supreme. So consumerism and selfishness run rampant. It's a licence to pollute.' She abruptly sat down.

An American man stood up without giving his name. 'This has gotten farcical. I didn't come here to receive a political lecture from liberals.' He stormed out.

Bruce shouted after him, 'If you can't stand the heat...'

The mumblings of discontent were getting louder. Dr Belstead tried to calm things down. 'Yes, we should definitely put some constraints on our future developments.'

Awhina was on her feet again. 'There are only two constraints at present: financial and political. Finance takes no account of safety or morality. It invests where the short-term profits are. As for any legal or political constraints, forget it. Selfless co-operation to tackle world-wide threats isn't a priority. Mechanisms for serious international collaboration aren't there. Men are hard-wired for tribalism and confrontation.'

By this time, Dr Belstead had lost all control. A man with a German accent was having a fierce argument with his neighbour.

Awhina was determined. 'Civilisations collapse because of a weakness which was there all along. Ours is an unwillingness to say no.'

The ship's purser intervened. He signalled to Dr Belstead, touching his watch.

'I'm afraid my allotted time is up.' It was hard to tell whether he was relieved or disappointed. 'I had hoped we might be able to talk about smart cities, virtual reality, and virtual assistants, but the clock has defeated us. Thank you all for coming. I hope it's at least got you thinking about what technology has to offer in these extraordinary times, and some of the challenges.'

David came straight up to Awhina. 'Well done, I thought you were magnificent. There's just one problem. I was going to ask you what you're doing tomorrow, but you've just said there is no tomorrow.

There is this evening, though. How about a stroll along the beach?'

....

They were paddling through lapping water as warm as a bath. Awhina's body was fighting her head, and both were in turmoil about David. Being touched by him, even just holding hands, felt strange. She was trying to decide, but conflicting thoughts were jamming up her brain. Should she? Did she want to? And if so, when? Did she need more time? If so, why? The thought that she might leave the pace to David never occurred to her.

'Have you heard from your mother?' That wasn't romantic, but then Awhina was trying to think practically, not romantically. Her feelings towards David had been warm and comforting, but also a bit more than that. She was enjoying the cruise immensely, but it was thinking about David which excited her when she woke up each morning. Now she felt she was at a crossroads, and she needed to be rational. That had temporally driven any romantic thoughts from her mind.

'She seems ok. They're keeping her in for a few days more for tests.'

'So about tomorrow. There's a trek to visit another tribe, the Wangoda, or we could go diving off the reef. Unless, of course, you'd rather be alone.'

If she'd been thinking straight, she might have marvelled at how he managed to put that with both modesty and confidence. Here was another decision she needed to make. 'You choose.'

'All right, let's visit the tribe. Then we'll be together all day. Under water, we'd be lucky if we got more than glimpses of each other pouting and bubbling and making moaning noises through our tubes.'

....

She was staring a few metres ahead of her as they walked. The water was sliding between her toes as she paddled. Some parrots were squabbling up in the trees to her right, but she hardly noticed them. He swung her gently round, and then brought her in against him. He kissed her, and she felt his hands slide around the backs of her hips. The kiss was long and moist, but she wasn't enjoying it. Her brain was thinking when her body was meant to be surrendering. Her plan, such as it was, had dipped out of sight. She placed her hands on his chest and pushed him away. She stood back, panicking. Her plan came back, so she reached out, spreading her hand firmly over his crotch. She instantly realised that the gesture had been demeaning. She was revolted with herself, with him. She took another step back, stared at him as though she'd done something intimate with the wrong person by mistake, turned, and ran back towards the ship. She went straight to her cabin and stayed there. She ordered a ham and cheese sandwich and ate it sitting on her bed. Even her balcony seemed to offer too much exposure.

Later that night, when she'd forced her disgusted self to analyse what had happened, she realised the absurdity of the sequence: push him away, stand back, hand forward, grope. His look of astonishment had told her how inappropriate it had been. She struggled to remember whether he had recoiled or not. How long had her hand remained there? Two seconds, five, surely not ten? Had she withdrawn because of his reaction? Or was it her horror at her own clumsiness? Or revulsion at his body and hers?

Why did it matter now? Surely whether she should abandon the cruise was more important? But it did matter. Why? Because she was desperately trying to replay it in her mind, over and over, in the hope that it might suddenly reveal itself to have been not that bad after all. The repetition, like counting sheep, must have made her fall asleep.

....

She realised she couldn't hide indefinitely, so she might as well face up to her shame now. She'd at last rationalised the incident in her mind. She'd intended, on the beach, to give David a sign that she was willing to contribute to their growing intimacy. That had been her plan, perhaps still could be. What had gone wrong was that a moment of doubt had made her fluff her performance.

She'd expected him to either avoid her or be cold. To her surprise, he and Bruce had sat down with her at breakfast, without asking if they could join her. Although David's 'good morning' had been a bit formal, she'd been grateful that his behaviour towards her seemed natural and relaxed, even if most of his conversation had been with Bruce. She wondered what Bruce had been told. She got the impression that everything Bruce said was with the aim of impressing her. Although she didn't admire that, his blather at least avoided the problem of what to say to David.

She'd failed to book herself onto the visit to the tribal village, so David used his charm to get her included. Before they set off, they had a pep talk from their guide.

'The Wangoda allow us to visit on several conditions. They believe that photography steals their souls, so no cameras or phones, please. You may look at the Wangoda, but please don't hold eye contact with any one individual for more than a few seconds. I will guide you quite close to them, but please don't go within ten feet of anyone. This is for the very practical reason that they are susceptible to diseases brought in from outside. Don't worry about gifts; that's all been dealt with as part of your package. And one more thing: please don't talk amongst yourselves or to me when you're with them. You can ask me as many questions as you like on the way, or after we've left.'

Awhina was pleased when David walked with her on the way to meet the Wangoda. She accepted his company, and Bruce's presence made it easy for her not to say much. She was determined not to apologise for last night. She thought she owed David an explanation, but she didn't think he'd want to hear it. Anyhow, Bruce's chatter prevented it, and time might be a healer during the rest of the day.

It was humid on the walk, so that Awhina kept

blowing out her cheeks and flapping her hands in front of her face.

'Here, take this.' David gave her his bush hat, and she fanned herself with it. He held her hand as they had to tread carefully over some slippery, moss-clad boulders. She didn't mind. They passed several waterfalls and some spectacular flowers with scarlet bracts tipped with yellow. The guide pointed out a Wilson's Bird of Paradise flying out of a distant tree, but Awhina had been holding David's hat in front of her face, so she didn't see it. As they climbed, views across the island kept appearing and disappearing. She could see a cone-shaped volcano and wondered when it had last erupted.

After an hour and a bit, their guide told them to rest. He handed out water to those who'd failed to bring any. They walked on for another half-hour until they could see some thatched houses ahead. The translator went on and disappeared into one of them. Ten minutes later, there was a long whistle. The translator reappeared, accompanied by a man, two women, and two children. Further tribespeople came out of other huts, about twenty in all. The two groups, natives and tourists, stood facing each other.

It was hard to remember not to stare at them. Awhina did stare. She was surprised to find that the women were fully clothed when she'd anticipated bare breasts. Their dresses were ankle-length, with intricate patterns, mainly of black, brown, and dark red. Their coal-black hair trailed down to their waists behind their backs. They stood gracefully with their weight on one hip, not what she'd expected. Their headbands were plain. The men were similarly clad, except that their sarongs came down only just below their knees. Each wore a broad belt and carried a longbow. The most startling thing about the men was their headdresses. Racemes of feathers soared up from their cone-shaped hats. The young girls were dressed like their mothers, except that they wore tasselled adornments on their heads. The boys were like their fathers, but their chests were more exposed. Everyone had bare feet. There was no sign of any infants.

Later, back at the ship, opinions would differ as to where the monkey came from. Some said it came from behind where the Wangoda were standing. Others said it had burst from the bushes at the side. One know-all said that it couldn't have been wild, because there weren't any monkeys on that island.

What was certain to all was that it charged at them with a long, loping, sideways run. A woman screamed, one called out, 'No, no, no,' and most of the group recoiled, one man falling sideways into a puddle. Very few stood still, but two who did were David and Awhina. The monkey stopped directly in front of them, bared its teeth, and hissed. David put an arm out towards Awhina in a protective gesture, but otherwise both remained still.

Two Wangoda men ran towards the group, causing further panic. About six of the tourists turned and ran down the path, back the way they'd come, shouting in fear. The monkey had shot off into the undergrowth. The Wangoda men stood glaring at the group, only ten feet from Awhina and David, who still didn't flinch. Bruce took out his phone and took some photos. The two tribesmen shook their bows at him, turned, and ran back towards the village in a peculiar leaping gait, letting out high-pitched yells as they did so. The remainder of the Wangoda had melted back into their huts.

On the walk back, a man came up to Awhina and David, quoting Kipling. '"If you can keep your head when all about you are losing theirs..." I thought you two were magnificent. If you hadn't stood your ground, the whole lot of us might have been off down the hill with arrows in our backs.'

David laughed. 'We didn't fancy ending up in the pot, mate.' Awhina felt good when he squeezed her hand and looked admiringly into her eyes. Later he would joke that every one of the instructions in the pep talk had been broken: keep your distance, don't stare at them, don't talk, and no photos. The only grey area was whether anyone had asked any questions, but as one man had called out, 'What the fuck?' they concluded that that rule too had been broken.

When they got back, she found a message asking her to see the ship's doctor.

'Your mother's made a full recovery, I'm glad to say. All the tests for tropical diseases have been negative. She's being discharged tomorrow morning, but due to a storm forecast for the Sulawesi region, we won't be able to get her back onto the ship for another couple of days.'

Two more days. Should she go for it? It's now or never, she told herself. So, you're terrified, you're far from certain that you want it, but you can't go through life wondering whether you should have tried. Bite the bullet, grasp the nettle, stop thinking in platitudes, you muffin. Concentrate, then go for it. You haven't got time. Decide now. Awhina did decide.

They were strolling along the upper deck after dinner. Bruce had gone on ahead of them. Awhina bundled David behind a bulkhead, threw her arms around his neck, and kissed him on the mouth. It only lasted a few seconds. But she made sure it would seem passionate. 'Come to my cabin. I want you for the night.'

David leaned back and peered at her. 'Are you sure?'

'Totally, absolutely, positively. Come soon after nine. I'll be waiting for you. You'd better get back to Bruce now.'

. . . .

When she returned to her cabin, she found she'd received a text from a leading physicist at Oxford, Dr Pheen Khodan. "I've read your essay on Dollen's Theory of Consequential Lensing. I think it's brilliant. You seem to have gained a complete insight into the thinking behind it, and you've also submitted some startling new possibilities. The man himself wants to meet you in London on the 28th. He says he's spotted an error in one of your calculations. Can you make it? I guess he wouldn't want to see you if he wasn't impressed. Or perhaps he's uncertain enough to want to get behind your thinking. Anyhow, it's an opportunity I don't think you should miss. Please let me know by return."

Recognition at last, and from one of the world's

greatest living physicists. It was a moment in her life when Awhina knew immediately that her self-confidence had been justified. She realised there was no way she could be there on the 28th. The ship would be somewhere in the region of West Papua by then. She started to text Khodan back, but the wi-fi had failed. After a short session of swearing, she left her cabin in search of the ship's purser.

'It happens now and then. We're passing close under some cliffs, so the connection to the satellite has been lost. We should be clear of the obstruction soon, and then we'll regain our link to Inmarsat.'

Twenty-five minutes until David was due. Just time to go through her calculations again to see where Dollen might have spotted the error, if there was one. She couldn't see it, although she was worried about an unsubstantiated assumption which she'd overlooked. Perhaps that was what he was referring to. By the time she'd looked through it all again and had decided that she hadn't made a mistake, it was five to nine. Then she remembered she needed to send that text about the meeting, asking if it could be postponed. She dashed it out, thankful that the wi-fi was working at last. It was now three minutes past. Panicking and swearing out loud, and with formulae still coursing through her brain, she changed into a simple smock dress. She'd decided earlier that sitting in her nightie would be too forward. Rather, let him undress her. She assumed that would be what he would want.

She was trembling like a gerbil. Some of it was excitement, some fear. She'd told herself earlier that the foreplay would be positive, whatever might come after. She'd ordered some champagne and two glasses, which had already been delivered. Now all she could do was wait, try to stay calm, stop thinking of the meeting with Dollen, and kick those fucking formulae out of her head. So far she wasn't succeeding.

The quiet knock on the door came ten minutes after nine. She was concentrating so hard on her breathing that she didn't look at him. But when she noticed that he too had brought champagne and two glasses she smiled, still looking at the floor. He kissed her lightly on the forehead. They sat down on the two cabin chairs, which she'd placed side by side. They made small talk, reliving the visit to the Wangoda. That helped, because they'd both been a bit heroic there together. They drank his bottle of champagne, and she felt herself relaxing. But when he placed his hand on hers, which was resting on her thigh, she tensed. She knew she was experiencing the first sensation of something, but what? Apprehension? Fear? Excitement? Arousal?

'I've never done this before.' There, she'd said it.

He looked at her kindly. 'If you mean what I think you mean, I'm surprised. You're highly desirable in every way. In fact, you're beautiful. There's a first time for everything. We'll do it slowly, at your pace, taking as long as you want.' He stood up and then knelt in front of her. He ran his hands slowly down the outside of her thighs, then turned them inwards and upwards, lifting up her smock. She felt little shockwaves jittering through her body. He kissed her on the mouth, tenderly and softly, pausing, releasing, then continuing. His eyes were kind, examining her face with his dependable smile. Before she knew it, his hands had slid under her bottom, and she felt herself being pulled upright.

She was panicking, but she couldn't speak to ask him to slow down. She forced herself to look at him. She could feel his skin becoming hotter and could see sweat on his forehead. Slowly, he started to lift her smock over her head. She felt she didn't want to co-operate, but she couldn't help herself, so she raised her arms, until the smock was clear and he could drop it onto the floor. He took a step forward so that they were just touching. His hands came up and cupped her breasts, then started to move down across her belly. Her leg muscles tightened. She felt herself shivering, in spite of the heat. She tried to step back, but her chair was in the way. Although her eyes were looking at the floor, she could see him undo the belt of his trousers, and then his zip. But the horror only came when she forced herself to look at his nakedness. Without even a gasp, she shimmied to her right and ran into the bathroom. She snatched at a towel, her mother's actually, and clutched it to her chest. She was about to run out of the cabin before she realised that she couldn't. She was trapped between her own nakedness and his. She darted towards the balcony, then realised that she couldn't go there either. It was overlooked by a neighbouring couple who were leaning out over a rail. There was nowhere for her to go. She faced him and flung her arms out in a gesture of despair, then crossed them over her chest and doubled up, rolling her thighs inwards to hold the towel in place over her pubic area.

David started putting on his clothes. She found the silence unbearable. He wasn't being unreasonably slow, but the seconds dragged. What was he going to say? He looked at her neutrally, turned, and quietly left the cabin without saying a word. She fell onto her bed, sobbing.

....

She was realistic enough to know that it was over between her and David. He wouldn't want a third attempt; he'd be disgusted with her by now. She was fairly certain that the same thing would happen again if they tried. He'd clearly ghosted her, and she was relieved. She'd taken to entering the dining room late, and assumed she was doing the right thing by not joining him and Bruce. She checked to see what activities they'd signed up to, and deliberately chose something different. She went down into some caves and kayaked up lagoons between mangroves, where a snake dropped out of a tree into the water behind her. In two days' time, they would be sailing into the waters to the west of Papua.

Now she had a new problem: Bruce. At first she thought he was acting as an ambassador on behalf of David. He kept coming up to her, and when he did so, she simply walked away. Soon it became clear from his lecherous smile that he was after her for his own ends. She felt abused by him and angry with David, feeling that she'd been "passed on", discarded, second-hand goods.

The next morning, Bruce caught her out by

returning to the restaurant while she was having breakfast. He sat down opposite her. 'Mind if I join you?'

She felt like saying that he should have asked that before he'd sat down, but she wasn't going to honour him with a reply. She gave him her frozen stare, then returned to her yoghurt.

'Fancy a walk along the cove after you've finished eating?'

'No.'

'Look, Athena. I'm sorry it hasn't worked out between you and David. But we might as well move on, and I'm here to help you. There's way over half the cruise still to go, and I don't like to see you not enjoying yourself.'

She ignored him, finished her meal, and left him to his babble.

Most of her thoughts and some of her emotions were poured into her work. She debunked Dr Anwazi's theory on the black hole information paradox and tore into Tigran Aslanyan's treatise on dark matter, before realising that it was a hoax. She declined an invitation to the fancy dress competition. When a fellow passenger jokingly told her that it was compulsory, she believed him, but she got the date wrong, causing a sensation by appearing in the bar before dinner, dressed scantily as a butterfly. She quickly retired to her cabin to change. A couple were playing chess in the lounge. Awhina stood over them, so that they shifted uneasily in their seats. After watching them for a couple of minutes she said, 'Knight to C5' and walked away.

Out on deck, Bruce came up to her again. 'When's my little butterfly going to spread her wings?' She glared at him and moved off. Captain Hasegawa was standing high up on the bridge, so she waved to him. He remained motionless before turning away. She wasn't sure whether he'd seen her or not.

Her mother was returning later that day, and Awhina was almost glad. She hadn't booked any activities, so she decided to go for a swim in the sea. She walked along the beach, clambered over some rocks, and found herself in a delightful little cove. There were low cliffs on either side, bracketing a narrow inlet. She sat down on the sand, barely a hundred metres across, and looked out at a large island only a couple of miles away. Just visible to the right, a great number of birds were diving into the sea. Climbing up onto a bluff to get a better look, she found a ledge and sat down. The water where the birds were diving was churning, though whether from tidal currents between the islands or from fish, she couldn't tell. She wondered whether she'd ever sat in a more beautiful spot, which she had all to herself. A lone bird with sweptback wings was riding the thermals above her head. She leant back, mesmerised, as she watched it circle. The sun was hot on her cheeks, but the heat was relieved by a soft breeze. The bird seemed to represent all that she was feeling: lone and free, soaring clear above the world. She closed her eyes. Her mind and her breathing slowed. She sensed the ground falling away. She was floating high above the cliff with the bird and then drifting out into the strait. Dollen's hypothesis,

Professor Coulter, Adam, Lily, her mother, David: they all seemed to swirl in a firmament of blue. Opening her eyes, she flung her head back and blinked at the sky. She rotated her shoulders in a rolling motion. She felt free, far from anyone, and at peace.

Her feeling of lonely pleasure was disturbed by a movement on the beach. She swore out loud. 'What the actual fuck!' She could see Bruce searching the cove. He must have followed her. She realised that if he looked up to where she was sitting, she would be on his horizon. Getting ready to crawl away, she put her hand on something yucky and involuntarily straightened. The movement must have caught his eye because he looked up, then started to clamber towards her. She felt a mixture of fury and a sense of violation that he was daring to think that he could share this spot which she'd found for herself. She looked out towards the other island, the diving birds, the turbulent water. She wanted to be there but knew she couldn't. She looked down. The swirling blue fringed with white foam, the freshness of the swell, they seemed so near, so within her reach, enticing her. Her head was floating, but in a nice way. Bruce was getting nearer. Not realising what she was doing, she stood up. She peeled off her blouse and stepped out of her jeans. Not even glancing at Bruce, now only a few metres away, she put her hands together and thrust them forward, tucked her head in, pushed out from the rock, and plunged.

Even though the height had been around thirty feet, she entered the water cleanly. Gravity and momentum took her naturally deep, but she streamlined her posture, and the quality of her dive meant that she slid through the water rapidly and smoothly. Fizzing pressure thrilled in her ears as she started to level out. Something ripped through her face. She felt a huge warmth flowering across the front of her head, followed by an intense stinging. She burst through the surface, gasping for air. Still exhilarated by what she'd done, she was puzzled to see a bloom of red expanding out across the water around her.

Bruce could see it too. What he could also see, and Awhina could not, was that she was being swept along the channel at the speed of someone jogging. He called out to her once but knew there was nothing he could do to help her. He half-ran, half-tumbled down onto the first beach, and dashed across it. Had he looked back over his shoulder at that moment, he might have seen something happen to Awhina which could have made a difference. But he didn't. He jumped and slipped over the boulders until he was on the larger beach, then put his head down and sprinted towards the jetty and the ship.

Now it seemed to Awhina that she'd had acid flung onto her face. Treading water, she put a hand up to her mouth and felt a huge flap of flesh fall to one side where her lower lip should have been. She looked up at the shore and realised it was moving. The water was warm, no problem there. She was too intelligent to start to struggle. The panic only came when she realised that she was bleeding heavily in shark-infested waters. She wasn't concussed, because she hadn't hit anything large, only sharp.

What she didn't know was that, as she'd levelled out, something razor-thin had sliced through her face, tearing it open. What she also didn't know yet was that a great gash like a living canyon extended from the side of her nose to the tip of her chin.

PART III

Bok had been up since before dawn. It was nearly time for him to return home with his younger brother Duk. Although his catch had been the best for several weeks, it was nothing like what it had been a few years back. Pollution, over-fishing, climate change; it could be a combination of any of those, but he couldn't do anything about it, so he just kept fishing. This time it was off the island of Sundabang. He told Duk he was going to have one more go just off the small headland at the mouth of a narrow bay. He'd noticed pelicans diving into the water half a mile offshore. His Yamaha 250hp motor was powerful, but even so he never risked the main channel between the two islands when the tide race was running, as it was now.

He was approaching the headland when Duk cried out. Bok could see him pointing ahead and to starboard, gesticulating, turning back to him, and then staring out again. Now Bok could see it too, someone in the water no more than two hundred metres away. It wasn't in the centre of the tide race, but far enough in for an approach to be hazardous. Bok didn't hesitate. He swung round to the right, cried out to his brother to grab the boathook, placed the boat downstream from the corpse, and put the engine into neutral. He'd done it skilfully. The body, which Bok could now see was alive, would drift seconds later down the starboard beam. He joined Duk at the side and threw a rope across the path of what he could now see was a woman. If they didn't succeed quickly, the current would spin the boat, and since neither Bok nor Duk was at the helm, they wouldn't be able to correct it quickly. They could rush back to the stern, turn the boat around, power it back to a position in front of her again, and try to repeat the process. But by that time she might be dead. They needed to move fast, all within seconds, and they did. Bok saw the woman grab the rope and cling on. The pull of the tide was massive, but because Bok had put the engine into neutral, the boat was moving at approximately the same speed as she was. Duk tried to snag the hook over the rope but missed. His second attempt succeeded. He saw her grasp the shaft with her other hand. The momentum swung her round, and she banged her head against the side of the boat. But Bok had her by the arm, and then Duk by the shoulders, so between them they pulled her aboard.

Bok needed to make two decisions and make them fast: how to treat this horrific-looking creature, and where to take her.

Bok lived between two worlds. He had left his tribe the Walukek nine years previously, followed by his brother Duk. To the extent that he was a fisherman with a smart boat, he had become a modern Papuan. But he still respected the customs of his tribe and was suspicious of many of the institutions of the twenty-first century, including hospitals. His departure from his tribal village high up in the interior had caused some hostility at first, but he had placated the elders by promising to bring them salted and dried fish, a pledge which he had honoured. He had maintained a good relationship with his shaman, whom he regarded as the best physical and spiritual healer he was ever likely to meet. Rather than return to the village where he lived now, a mere twenty minutes away, Bok told Duk to steer a course to the south, towards the mainland where his tribe dwelt. It would take them an hour and a half to get there. He realised that the woman could well bleed to death by then, but he knew what he must do to try to prevent it.

He assembled what he needed. It was fortunate that he had two completely clean cloths. He took his sharpest knife and rinsed it in seawater. Then he took the biggest fish he'd caught that day, a juvenile grey reef shark. It had the advantage of a tough skin. He looked down at his patient, his compassion fighting his revulsion at the ghastly sight of her distorted face. She really was repulsive to look at. Her nose had been torn away on one side, and a huge fissure had been slit into her left cheek and down to her chin. But it was her lips which were so horrendous that his eyes were drawn to them with a terrible fascination. The upper one had merely been torn open, but the lower had been ripped apart, so that it hung in two divergent flaps of flesh. She was still bleeding heavily, and his first task was to staunch the flow of blood. Mopping at it would do no good; it would simply keep on coming. He needed to bind it, and he knew what with.

He slit open the shark to reveal its vast liver. He cut strips of skin, scraped the flesh off the backs, and laid them to one side. Then he sliced thin pieces of liver of varying sizes. He started placing them in the trenches in the woman's face. She yelped and squirmed, and then started screaming. He slapped her across the neck, not daring to hit her face. He then talked soothingly to her, and she subsided. He kept speaking while he laid the strips of sharkskin transversely across the wounds, hoping they would bind with the liver and her congealing blood. Doing the same with her lower lip was impossible; it had been sundered too far apart. Any supporting liver underneath would make her gag, and she would probably swallow it and choke. He took one of the clean cloths and called across to Duk to join him. While Bok placed some liver across her lower lip, and then covered it with a much larger piece of sharkskin, Duk immediately wrapped it in the dry cloth, and between them they bound it quickly around her head. Unable to breathe, she moaned, until Bok cut a slit in front of her nostrils. Finally, he took the other clean rag, washed it in seawater, wrung it out, and tied it over the first cloth. He patted her soothingly on the hand and, for the first time in twenty minutes, looked up.

Inspektur Polisi Satu Jadibata pondered the disappearance of Awhina Fernandez. It didn't seem a difficult case. If, as the Australian had told him, she'd dived into the waters of the Straits of Sundabang, then she wouldn't have lasted long. The man had given the time as 10.30 in the morning, which was approximately half an hour after several witnesses had seen her walking along the beach away from the ship. Having consulted the tide tables and talked to some locals, Jadibata concluded that the current had been at its strongest half an hour later. If Ms Fernandez had managed to avoid being dragged under, her struggles would soon have attracted the attention of sharks. The Australian had reported seeing blood in the water around her head. That might indicate that she'd received a fatal wound, perhaps had already died. In any case, the sharks would soon have picked up the scent of blood and would have homed in on her.

He was duty-bound to take into consideration the fact that the Australian was the only witness to her diving into the sea. Murder, although unlikely, couldn't be ruled out. Through an interpreter, he questioned several of the passengers on the ship. Some had noticed Awhina talking to Bruce recently and had assumed that they'd struck up a friendship. David confirmed this. No motive could be pinned on Bruce. Jadibata walked with him to the low cliff from which Awhina had dived. He could see the imprints of what seemed to be her bare feet in the grit. There was no sign of a struggle. Everything stacked up. His boss was pressuring him to release the ship, and he could see no reason to detain it. The case would remain open for another few weeks in case a body was reported washed up onshore anywhere. Jadibata thought it extremely unlikely. He spent part of those weeks visiting remote settlements, both on Sundabang and its neighbour. But he knew he was wasting his time.

....

The tribe which Bok had left nine years ago, the Walukek, lived mainly inland. They were accessed from the sea by a path which rose steeply from a small fishing village and then levelled out onto a plateau. The village on the beach lay in a small bay half a mile wide. Every single house was on stilts, half of them built out over the sea and the others over the sand. There were about forty houses in total in a cluster down one end, all except one, which was isolated at the far end of the bay. It too stood on stilts at the end of a long walkway over the sea, almost a pier. The whole area was hemmed in by steep jungly cliffs.

There was only one person who could save the woman's life. Bok needed to get her to his spiritual mentor, Umpanu, quickly. There was just one problem. Because Umpanu had one wife on the coast and another inland, it was a gamble that he would be at the water's edge today. Travelling on foot was the only way to get from one of his villages to the other. It took just under two hours to make the journey. Bok had staunched some of the flow of blood, but even the outer cloth bound across the woman's face was now oozing dark red. In this heat and humidity, infection would soon take hold, if it hadn't already. She would be unlikely to recover from a further two hours' delay, if Umpanu was in his other village inland.

As Duk grounded the boat onto the beach, Bok leapt from the prow. He ran to a little kiosk, shouting for Umpanu. The woman inside pointed. Bok twisted round and then sprinted towards one of the houses. He burst in and gabbled out his story. Before he'd finished, Umpanu had risen to his feet. He calmly put a hand on Bok's shoulder, smiled reassuringly at him, and walked out of the house towards the boat.

. . . .

Diane Fernandez's helicopter had taken her back to Sundabang from Sulawesi. She had fully recovered. As she stepped aboard the ship, she was pleased to be greeted at the top of the gangway by Captain Hasegawa himself. She was only slightly concerned when he led her to his cabin and asked her to be seated. He told her the news that her daughter had not been seen for eight hours.

'That girl is always doing something eccentric. I expect she's jumped off a cliff, or something.'

Captain Hasegawa coughed politely. 'She has.' He told her Bruce's story and how the police were looking into it. He didn't mention the strength of the current, nor that Bruce had seen blood around her head, nor the shark-infested waters. He wondered whose job it was to tell her those things. This woman in front of him seemed remarkably calm, too calm. He was tempted to give her some more of the facts but decided that would panic her unnecessarily and most likely cause a scene. He had his other passengers and the reputation of the shipping company to think of.

'I feel sure that the police are doing everything they can to locate your daughter, Mrs Fernandez.' He postponed telling her that he would soon be forcing a decision from her: whether to stay on the island, fly back to the UK, or continue with the cruise. He hoped it wouldn't be the latter.

It was only when David came up to her that Diane learnt that Bruce had seen Awhina dive. Bruce was summoned and told her the whole story as he had seen it. When David put a hand on her arm, she turned helplessly towards him.

'She's gone, hasn't she?' Diane started crying.

'I'm afraid it looks like it. We've been told that the chances of surviving in those waters for more than half an hour or so are virtually zero. I'm so very, very sorry. She was a lovely girl.'

Next morning, a steward requested Diane's attendance in Captain Hasegawa's cabin.

'Mrs Fernandez, I believe you know that the chances of finding your daughter alive are now very slim. I offer my condolences on behalf of all my crew. As you know, we are due to sail this evening. There are several choices open to you. You are welcome to sail with us, you can stay on Sundabang to assist the police, or we can arrange for you to fly home. The last two options would have to be co-ordinated through your travel insurance company. If you decide to stay on the island, we have an agent who can look after you. The only decision I need now is whether you wish to continue with the cruise, or not.'

Diane was too distraught to make a full decision, except that she spat back at him, 'No cruise,' and then broke down sobbing.

In the end, after the ship had sailed, she decided that she was wasting her time on Sundabang, so she booked a flight home.

. . . .

How Umpanu prevented infection from setting in, no one other than the healer himself would ever know. He never divulged his methods. Umpanu was not a shaman, nor was he a dokta, at least not one trained by the authorities. His skills had been passed down from his father. Was his treatment of Awhina spiritual, herbal, or chemical? Certainly herbal, perhaps a combination of all three.

Umpanu wasn't squeamish. He had seen and treated mangled faces, limbs, and torsos before. Throughout his twenty-five-year career, he'd treated the terrible wounds from arrows and spears when the Walukek had fought their enemy the Suamu by the old methods. The battles had been ritualistic, with young bloods competing to prove their bravery. Even so, deaths had occurred, and injuries were common. Worse were the more recent times when machetes had been used. The introduction of firearms had made the injuries and deaths even more horrific, and far more frequent. But both tribes had now pulled back from allowing their warriors to use guns or machetes. So the leaders of both tribes had managed to restrict fighting to the traditional methods in recent years.

Umpanu examined his patient. She was tall, but perhaps no taller than the many foreign tourists he'd glimpsed now and then. He admired her dark eyes which were mercifully unscathed. He'd never seen a pair so round. Her skin, where it hadn't been mutilated, was as smooth as polished stone. It was less creased than a Papuan's, but with its colour of fertile earth freshened by rain, the pigmentation could easily pass off as that of a woman of his own tribe, the Walukek. But the way those eyebrows arched so dramatically was distinctly from somewhere else; he couldn't guess where.

Umpanu gave her an anaesthetic drink which knocked her out. After a few minutes he started to remove each of Bok's fishy dressings one at a time, assessing the severity of each section of the wound. He worked from the nose down. Her nostril had been sliced on the left so that a tongue of flesh was hanging out to the side. The trench below as far as her upper lip, although deep, was clean and even. He treated it and moved on to her mouth. It was shocking, even for someone as experienced as Umpanu. The upper lip had been split open, and the incision had been so deep that a tooth and gum had been damaged. The bottom lip was far worse. It dangled open in two flaps, the softness of the tissue making each fillet hang down separately towards her chin. The blade of metal, coral, or whatever it had been, had sliced so deep that it had cut through her gum, and had partly removed a tooth, which he would soon have to extract. Her tongue too had been slit, although he was confident that it would heal without permanent damage, if she survived at all. The fissure between her lower lip and chin, like the injury between her mouth and nose, was clean. The incision to her chin was slight.

It was now obvious to Umpanu that the blow, swipe, or whatever it had been, had entered at her nose and concluded at her chin. Because the force had been down onto her upper lip, as opposed to against it, that had merely been sliced open. But the object had clearly wrenched against her lower lip. Instead of just cutting it, the thing had pulled at it and torn it open. Whatever had caused the injury had been thin and razor sharp. Anything thicker or heavier would have killed her outright.

Now Umpanu had to do two things: prevent infection from gaining a hold and sew up the wounds as best he could. With luck and potent treatment, he might be able to save her life. But her disfigurement would be severe and permanent.

. . . .

Awhina lay on her couch and gingerly put a hand to her face. Although she didn't know it, thirteen days had passed since Bok had delivered her to Umpanu. For the first ten she'd been heavily sedated, and during the periods when Umpanu had operated on her she'd been fully anaesthetised. All she'd known was darkness. Now she realised that the solid mask, which had been almost as hard as plaster of Paris, had been replaced by much softer bandages. She pressed her fingers carefully onto her face. Her left cheek felt numb, but when she pushed onto the area around her mouth, she let out a cry of pain and instantly withdrew her hand.

She'd been conscious enough in the last few days to recognise the two people who visited her. A woman came to serve her meals and wash her. Thick low eyebrows had made her seem severe at first, but when she looked down at Awhina, her eyelids wrinkled compassionately, and she smiled. Her voice was soft and soothing, although Awhina couldn't understand what she was saying. Sometimes she felt her hand being gently squeezed in what she took to be a friendly gesture. Sometimes it meant that her pulse was being taken.

Her other visitor seemed more like someone recollected from a dream. His visits were irregular, and sometimes she wondered whether she'd imagined him. He had a broad nose, deeply indented folds to his cheeks and, like the woman, low forbidding brows. Yet somehow his presence was reassuring.

Gradually, Awhina was becoming conscious of her surroundings. She was dressed in a plain linen nightie, and she was lying on a low couch, little more than a foot off the ground. Her mattress was made of what felt like rushes, covered with a sheet. There was a crudely made bedside cabinet, the only furniture apart from her bed. The room was a tightly shuttered box made of timber, wattle, and bamboo. Now, for the first time, she became aware of water gently lapping somewhere nearby. Her ears were ringing and her whole head seemed hot. The atmosphere around her was stifling, and the humidity oppressive. She drifted back to sleep.

She was awoken by a hand on her wrist. She looked up to see the woman smiling down at her. She realised that she was being pulled gently upwards. Feeling weak and slightly nauseous, she tried to stand, but she felt hands being placed firmly onto her shoulders to indicate that she was to do no more than sit. The woman walked across the room and opened the door, letting in a view of the last rays of a sunset, warm air being sucked in, and stifling humidity. The unfamiliar light made her screw up her eyes.

After she'd been sitting for five minutes or so, the woman, still smiling, pulled her by the hands again, and this time she did stand up. She felt her right arm being draped around the woman's shoulder for support. It was then that she realised that her nurse was barely five feet tall. They moved slowly towards the open air, Awhina now realising that her legs couldn't safely support her own weight. They stood on a small balcony, Awhina leaning groggily onto a rail. Her eyes were burning after so long in the dark. Gazing around, she could see other small huts on stilts clustered down the far end of a beach, bathed in the ochre light of the setting sun. Closer, low tables were covered with what looked like drying fish. Behind, a steep valley climbed up towards the hills. On either side, vertical cliffs draped in lush tropical vegetation rose for several hundred feet above the small bay. Even in her woozy state, Awhina could appreciate how exotic it looked.

The nurse pointed to where the sun had now set.

She turned to face the east and swung her arm up until it was vertical. Awhina instantly understood that she was indicating the following day by describing the sun's trajectory. She then pointed to Awhina's face and stroked her bandage. It was clear that it would be removed within the next twenty-four hours.

Later that night, after she'd eaten a meal of fish and puréed vegetables, she started to think where she might be and what had happened to her. For some reason which she struggled to understand, she either couldn't or didn't want to recall the recent past. Adam, Professor Coulter, and Lily were all quite vivid to her. She started thinking about her thesis, but when mathematical formulae swam in and out of her head, she became distressed and tried to dismiss them. She fell asleep thinking vaguely of a ship and a man and being able to windsurf, and then her mother came into the picture, but why?

....

She was aware of the man looking at her, gently feeling her face, giving a little grunt, and then departing. The nurse gave her a sweet-tasting drink. By the time she woke up, the day had passed and it was dark outside. Feeling a dull ache in the region of her mouth, she put a hand up to feel it, but the woman restrained her. She was given another drink and soon fell asleep.

The next day, her energy, enthusiasm, and memory had mostly returned. She could recall her thesis and remember most of her experiences on the cruise. But restrictions made her squirm with frustration. She missed having access to any electronic device, particularly the internet, or even the means to write anything down. Although her ability to hold information in her head had always been so outstanding as to be almost freakish, there was a limit to how much even she could develop her thoughts without recording them. As for her recollection of events, all was reasonably complete up to the time when she thought she'd walked up to a clifftop with David. She was failing to realise that she'd gone there to avoid someone, and it was Bruce who had appeared, not David. After that, she remembered nothing until a week ago. She speculated where she might be. She knew that the ship had been about to enter the islands off Papua New Guinea. What she didn't know was that she'd been taken by Bok from one of those islands to the mainland itself, and that this seaside village was in West Papua.

Feeling stronger, she walked out onto the balcony. She decided to see how far she might be able to walk along the beach, perhaps as far as the village. It was then that she realised there was a gate across where her balcony joined the pier, which she hadn't noticed when she'd stood there with the nurse two nights before. It was padlocked. She wondered whether she was a prisoner but preferred to think that the gate was there for her own protection. There was no danger of her falling into the water from the balcony, but the pier itself was only a narrow walkway made of loose and uneven planks, with no handrail on either side. Awhina had never been one to accept other people's restrictions. To her, that gate was a challenge.

So when the nurse came to retrieve her breakfast dishes, Awhina seized her by the arm and bundled her out onto the balcony. She pointed to the locked gate, shook her head vigorously, and made the motion of a key being turned.

'I need it open. Open it.'

The woman looked alarmed and shook her head. Awhina made a motion with her fingers, pointing first to the woman, then to herself, indicating the two of them walking together down the pier. When that produced no direct response, merely a pathetic look, Awhina linked their arms together and aggressively marched around the balcony, dragging the woman with her. The reaction she got was a distraught wail and a gesture that she should return to her room. Awhina decided she would wait by the gate until the woman was forced to open it, then barge her way through. But she had a better idea. She needed to think carefully. It was now clear that she was being held captive. She was a prisoner of the mysterious man who operated on her, with this woman as his accomplice. What Awhina needed to do was get to the village without causing a commotion, which meant ambushing the woman as she came in, somehow tying her up, taking the key, and letting herself out. It was now time to think of how to do that.

It never happened, because a new opportunity, a much better one, appeared before her eyes a couple of hours later. She was standing on the balcony, looking down at a shoal of fishes swimming through the piles, when she saw movement by the headland ahead of her. A small white yacht was gliding towards the centre of the bay, slowing all the time. She could see a woman at the stern operating the wheel, a man at the front looking as though he had his hands on an anchor, and a second woman in sunglasses and a yachting cap standing statuesquely towards the rear, surveying the scene. The boat stopped and the anchor was thrown overboard. Awhina realised she mustn't delay. If they went ashore quickly, her opportunity might be lost. There were only a hundred metres between her and the yacht.

She was wearing a smock which had been provided to her, and the same bra and panties she'd been wearing when she'd jumped off the cliff to avoid Bruce. She stepped out of the smock, crouched down, and swung her legs under the rail. Sitting for no more than a second or two, she launched herself feet-first into the sea. As she swam towards the yacht, she could see that the crew were preoccupied and hadn't spotted her. She swam right up to a few metres short of the hull, right by where the two women were standing. They were fair-skinned, talking in English. Treading water, she raised an arm.

'Hi'. The women turned towards her looking startled.

'Help!'

The effect on the woman at the wheel was instant. She shrieked, not a short piercing yelp, but a rhythmic, repetitive scream of prolonged terror. Awhina was so mesmerised by this reaction that she failed to notice the man leaning down and thrusting a hooked pole towards her face. Thinking he might have wanted her to grab it, she did so, only to find that he'd withdrawn it and was now ramming it painfully into her shoulder. His last thrust caught her in the mouth, tearing open her bottom lip. He shouted to the woman at the stern to start the engine, then ran to the prow. He hauled up the anchor, ran back again, and took over the controls. Engine roaring, the yacht started to move ahead and then swing away, leaving Awhina floundering in oily water and engine fumes. The last thing she noticed was the woman in the yachting cap leaning over the rail vomiting. It would be another three weeks before she would understand why.

PART IV

I'm daydreaming on a low wooden bench which they've made specially for me. The people I'm with mostly sit on the ground or squat on their haunches when it's wet. I've tried doing it so I can be one of them, but I need to build up my thigh muscles. I'm practising every day.

The houses behind me are on stilts, same as those by the sea. The ones for sleeping in, the men's separate from the women's, are round, with entrances so low I have to stoop almost double to get inside. Those used for keeping pigs, and for communal activities such as cooking, are rectangular. There's bird song all around, although the men sometimes whoop and whistle, so it's hard to know who's calling. The smells are of woodsmoke, body sweat, and pig shit.

I think I must be among some of the most primitive and exotic people in the world. Their faces are painted, and they wear so much bling that they rustle and clack when they move. The men look fierce with all their feathers and bones, but I'm not scared of them.

I'm pleasantly tired and elated. Today was the first day when I was allowed to go out to work in the fields with Yaku, Ekapamne, and some of the other women. I was given a wooden tool with a broad end like a paddle, set at a right angle. I think it would be called a mattock back home. One end of the handle was pointed. When I asked what that was for, Ekapamne made thrusting motions all around her, and the other women laughed. It must be for defence, although against what I don't yet know. We were harvesting sweet potato and taro. I've been told the heart-shaped leaves of taro are poisonous if eaten raw, but they can be cooked. As for the roots, they're naturally earthy and nutty, and my people have lots of different ways of cooking them.

As well as taro and sweet potato, we eat breadfruit, cassava, various leaves which I haven't got to know yet, plantain, and pork on special occasions. Pigs aren't just food; they're currency. I've been told a man can buy a wife for ten pigs. How good a wife, I don't know. I wonder whether anyone's saving up their pigs to buy me? Actually, that's not funny. I don't yet know my role in this village, or why they seem happy for me to be here. OMG, are they fattening me up? For marriage? To be eaten? I certainly have been displaying porky tendencies since I got here.

Now I've been given some kava to drink while I

sit and watch the piglets and children scamper over the brushed soil. Every now and then one of the children darts up to me, freezes, and then runs away shrieking to its mates, who repeat the process. When bored with me, they dive at the piglets, who squeal in terror. A successful dive means that the child is dragged along in the dirt, and the sharp little hooves sometimes draw blood. Yesterday I tried to join in, but I hadn't noticed a stick on the ground. I slipped and landed slap on my buns. In pain from a bruised coccyx, I sat there screwing up my face in pain, which the children thought was an invitation to jump on me.

I've been up here in the hills for thirty-eight days. I know I have because I've kept a record by cutting notches into a piece of wood. Yaku's told me why I'm here in this inland village of the Walukek tribe. She's one of the two wives of Umpanu, the man who operated on me down on the coast. I'm naturally good at languages, and one of the reasons why I've been able to pick this one up so quickly is that Umpanu speaks a little broken English. I'm inland in West Papua, which is the western part of Papua. They're both on the island of Papua New Guinea. New Guinea is an independent country, whereas Papua is part of Indonesia. I remember that from Penelope's lecture on the ship. She said it was complicated. I think it's straightforward for anyone with a brain.

Yaku and I are good friends. She's very patient with me, which is another reason why I've picked up some of the language of the Walukek so fast. Yaku and I wear different clothes. She's married, so her dress is predominantly a rusty red, woven round her body. Because I'm single, I wear a tassel skirt made of tree bark. Yaku showed me the palm it comes from. I think it might be sago. My midriff and shoulders are bare, but I have a bib, which is a higher tassel similar to the one below, hanging over my shoulders and covering my breasts. It took a week or two to get used to it all, because I found it scratchy, but now it's very comfortable. These garments don't soak up water, which runs straight off, just as well in this climate, where the rain can be as heavy as a bathroom shower. I've learnt to enjoy the rain. It has an endlessly changing rhythm as it drums down onto the soil and rattles the leaves, making a sound like an audience clapping. I've also been given a hat, simple compared with everyone else's. It's a sort of brown skullcap but bigger, fringed with dull orange feathers. Most of the women, including Yaku, have strings of ornaments made from snail and cowrie shells, and even pig's teeth. Their headgear is more elaborate than mine, with black and bright red feathers. Ekapamne makes patterns on my face using a white clay.

Most of the women carry multi-coloured woven string bags called bilums wherever they go. They're used for carrying vegetables, fruit, firewood, and personal items. Some are huge, suitable for transporting children or even small pigs. Mine is smaller and plainer than most.

Walukek tools are made of stone, bone, pig's tusks, wood, and bamboo. I can't believe they haven't had some exposure to metal, but they don't use it much. Perhaps they simply want to preserve their traditional way of life.

. . . .

I now know why the woman on the yacht screamed at me. Yaku sat down beside me and gave me a cuddle. It's been a terrible shock, but at least it's given me a reason why I want to stay here with these people, who seem to accept me. Never taking her eyes off me, Yaku handed me a small and rather rusty mirror. I glanced down and nearly dropped it. The face which stared back at me wasn't just distorted and ugly, it looked evil. My nose turns up at the side which gives me a permanent sneer. A huge scar runs down from there to my chin. But it's my lips that are clapped the most. The upper one has a vertical slit, giving the impression of a mouthy frown. My lower lip is worse. It droops down, so that it looks like I'm sulking. So that was what the trio on the yacht had seen. If I were to return to my own people now, adults would be revolted by my appearance, children petrified. But here they seem to accept me as I am. I'm in no hurry to return. I think I'll make this my gap year.

Before my hunger for physics and mathematics became high-key obsessions, biology was my passion. Nature still fascinates me. This forest is a botanical paradise, and there are some seriously weirdo plants and creatures in it. Yesterday I took off by myself. I couldn't go far as it's easy to get lost. But Ekapamne had shown me a waterfall close by. The sound was full-on. I could hear but not see the tinkling of unseen rivulets below the carpet of leaf litter. Exotic calls made me swing round, looking for hidden birds: a creaking gate; a petulant screeching; large drops of water plinking from a great height into a pool; a honking like an impatient driver in a vintage car. These competed with the whistling and rasping of frogs and insects. The scents were equally varied, from rotting meat to divine nectar and stony minerality. Aromas of fecundity and decay mingled in the humid air. I recognised ginger, vanilla, orange juice, dung. Ahead of me, some white flowers looked like resting butterflies. When I started to move past them, they all took off, swirling, dancing, and then falling back to where they'd been. Enchanted, I laughed at the beauty of it all.

Nights are spooky. The women cough, splutter, and snuffle all through their sleep. I don't know whether it's because I'm unused to this diet, but I often have to get up to go for a wee in the night. If it's late, the forest is relatively quiet, which I find creepy. But earlier on there's a frightful din. Frogs and crickets are in full voice, and there seem to be so many of them. Flying foxes with their giant wingspans go thumping through the air and crashing into branches. When they return, it's a splatter-fest of liquid poo bombing down. Then there's a deep hollow booming sound which manages to seem far away and yet almost inside me. I can take all these sounds better than the silence.

I've known for a long time that something was seriously wrong with my mouth. I could feel it with my hand. My lower lip seemed to droop down in two ways at once and I'm missing a tooth. Eating has at times been difficult but I'm slowly getting better at it. Until recently, I'd had little reason to speak, but now when I do, my words sound fluffy, all the consonants being dependent upon my use of my tongue and teeth. I can only half-form the letters *b*, *p*, and *f* by giving a little puff of air. Even then, they sound more like a *t* or a *c*. The letters *m* and *v* are virtually impossible. So I use a lot of made-up sign language. The Walukek laugh when they don't understand me, but they never seem to get angry or frustrated.

Ekapamne's my sis. She's so cool. She's been given the job of showing me round and looking after me. She was a bit formal for the first few days until I punched her on the shoulder and winked at her. We've laughed together ever since. She's slightly smaller than me in every way, but her skin is exactly the same colour as mine. When I say its surface is perfect, I'm not exaggerating. It has a lightly oiled, polished, buffed-up look, shiny and yet textured. She lets me touch her on the arm, and sometimes I stroke her face. When I do, she laughs. She has a fringe of black braids and a similar headdress to mine. Across her forehead, below the fringe, a thin headband with two white feathers on either side of her eyes makes her look exotic. Her teeth are white, even, and in the right place. Many of the other women have large gaps between horribly stained teeth, so that their smiles are orangey-brown. Ekapamne's eyes, although large like mine, are permanently bloodshot. When I look at her nose, I think of the Tyrannosaurus's assessment of mine. Ekapamne's, like all the Walukeks', is so broad that the nostrils are like a scalene triangle. Her brows are low and severe, same as all her tribe's, but when she smiles and wrinkles those black eyes, I'm in heaven. Her skirt and bib have ornaments which I don't have, I guess to show her status as a married woman.

When I'd learnt enough of her language, she was able to quiz me. 'Have you got children? No? Are you married? Why not?'

I'm just as curious about her. She's only nineteen. She's married to one of the warriors. I enjoy bouncing her two-year-old son on my knee and laughing into his face. Like all the men except Umpanu, her husband takes no interest in me.

Today Ekapamne showed me how the Walukek harvest salt. She led me down to where water seeped out from below some cliffs. Mosses, fungi, and orchids so white that it looked like I was seeing them by moonlight, clustered at the gloomy entrance to a limestone grotto. A mouldy smell of rotting vegetation added to the feeling of decay. Ekapamne whispered that ghosts gathered there. It wasn't difficult to believe her. She showed me how plantain leaves had been left in the damp gravel to absorb the salt. After lifting them, she carefully folded them into wads and carried them back to the village. There she showed me leaves that were drying, and ash from others that had been burnt. It was the ash which contained the salt. It was kinda like, 'here's one I made earlier'.

When I'd learnt still more of the language, Yaku was able to tell me what had happened to me. After I'd been injured for the second time, when that head busta on his yacht had used a harpoon or whatever on me, some of the good work which Umpanu had been carrying out on my injuries had been undone. After he'd dressed my reopened wound, I was carried here.

I don't understand everything. I can now remember most things about the cruise: the excursions, the sports, the lectures, and the places we visited. I can recall my mother being helicoptered to hospital, but not her coming back. I can see two men, David and Bruce. I kissed David, but how far did we go with sex? Not all the way, I know that. There was something about it that was exciting but also unpleasant. How did I get to the mainland, that village on the beach? Yaku made waving motions with her hands, so I must have come from over the sea, but I have yet to find out why and who brought me.

. . . .

Inspektur Polisi Satu Jadibata had concluded his report. His half-hearted attempts to find Awhina Fernandez or her remains along the coast and in the villages across the sound had failed, as he knew they would. The only witness and the woman's mother had departed long ago. Jadibata's boss approved the closure of the case. Verdict: misadventure.

Because it was the long vac, none of Awhina's friends attended her memorial service. Most of those who were there, and there weren't many, were either relatives or friends of Diane's. Awhina's father turned up grudgingly, because he had a rush order for a customer in Dubai. A vicar gave a sermon which presented a portrait of Awhina as a fun-loving girl who studied hard but liked to party, hugely popular with her many friends. Had any of them been there, they might have wondered who he was talking about.

....

Professor Coulter's distaste was turning to anger. He didn't like being disturbed about work on holiday. As he read the email, he discovered that the subject was his nightmare of a student, Ms Fernandez. Worse, she was being eulogised.

"Dear Professor Coulter,

"I am sorry to be troubling you during the vacation, but I think you might be able to help me regarding an important matter. I understand that Ms Athena Fernandez is a student of yours, and by all accounts an outstanding one. I myself have read some of her papers, and they reveal an exceptional talent. You must be proud of her.

"I have been approached by Dr Pheen Khodan to try and trace Ms Fernandez. Dr Khodan says that she sent a text to her saying that Professor Dollen, no less, wanted to meet with her to discuss his Theory of Consequential Lensing. Ms Fernandez responded to the text immediately saying that she was in Indonesia and could not attend on the date proposed. That was over a month ago. She said that she would be willing to meet Dollen on another date. All subsequent texts, emails, and phone calls have remained unanswered.

"I am keen that someone of Ms Fernandez's obvious talents should not miss what looks like an opportunity to further what may become a brilliant career. Having failed with every form of electronic communication, I wonder if you could possibly give me her address, so that I may write to her?

Yours sincerely, (Dr) Christopher Timms"

It didn't take Coulter long to reply.

"Dear Dr Timms,

"Although I can confirm that Ms Awhina Fernandez is indeed a student of mine, I regret that both the GDPR and university procedures prevent me from disclosing her personal details to anyone.

Yours sincerely, Wyvern Coulter."

Dr Timms wondered why Coulter had called her Awhina. He checked the name on the papers she'd submitted to Professor Dollen. All were in the name of Athena Fernandez. Strange.

....

I've now been here for sixty-one days. I've learnt more of the language and customs. I feel this is where I belong, but something is disturbing me. It seems that the forest isn't the safe place I'd thought it was. I've been told that there's a huge badass bird out there taller than a turkey. It's highly aggressive, and its dagger-like claws can swipe your entrails out. I didn't believe it at first, thinking it must be just another of those scary spirits which the Walukek are always banging on about. But then Yaku showed me some huge black feathers half a metre long and some orange and blue skins. She said that the bird had only been caught a few days ago. Then she told me that a woman had been killed by one three years previously.

There are some nightmarish creepies up here in the forest. Ekapamne had obviously decided that this was the morning when she would scare the shit out of me. As we left the village, I couldn't believe how beautiful it was. Sunbeams, filtered by the trees, lit up the natural mist mingling with steam from the thatch and smoke from the fires. A pair of dragonflies were dancing around a low bush whose flowers were like flame-coloured candles. Water was dripping everywhere from the remains of a storm in the night. Somehow the smoke of human habitation seemed to complement the earthy scents rising from the forest floor. I sighed, but it was a sigh of pleasure. Ekapamne turned to laugh at me. She stopped and pointed to a tapering hole in the ground, then picked up a small stick and gently tweaked some white threads near the entrance. In steady jerking movements, a black tarantula emerged. It was bigger than my hand, bigger than anyone's hand, more like King Kong's. Then she told me that it wasn't the most dangerous spider. She said there was a highly poisonous one which lives in a tunnel and another which would jump on me. I thought she was joking, but I couldn't be sure. Further down the valley, we saw a giant lizardy thing the size of a small crocodile. Having my hand bitten off by strong jaws wouldn't be my only problem, she said. Poison would set in and reduce my flesh to jelly, to be sucked out by the monster.

Those aren't the only dangers. Yaku told me that a neighbouring tribe, the Suamu, are hostile towards the Walukek. They even fight each other. But it wasn't just what I'd been told that worried me. I could sense the nervousness when I was out in the fields with the women, the way they looked round, and the fact that there was always one of them who wasn't working but seemed to be standing guard.

This morning, it all came to a head. There was great excitement from dawn onwards. A warrior with his body and face smeared with a mixture of pig grease and ash came round the corner of a hut looking like a ghost. I squawked and leapt back in terror. He grinned and shook his spear at me, the shithole, before I could recover from my terror. More warriors came running out, adorned with bones, feathers, and goodness knows what else. Their eyes were surrounded by what appeared to be circles of ochre mud, making them look fierce and wild. They assembled, about forty of them, some carrying long spears, others bows with slender arrows. They hooted and yelled and stamped for ten minutes, and then they all sort of loped off along a path which led into the forest. The women and children all came out and watched them. They hadn't joined in the dancing, nor had they approached the men to wish them well, but gazed at them looking worried. I wanted to follow the men and see what happened, but Yaku stopped me. She told me that the men were off to join forces with some other Walukek villagers, and then they would all face the Suamu together. Arrows would fly, and anyhow women weren't allowed to watch the fighting.

Late in the afternoon, I heard chanting coming from the forest. It sounded happy, so I thought our boys must have slayed it. When they neared the village, they seemed to be dancing and smiling in triumph, but then I noticed two stretchers and one large bag which looked as though it contained a body. It did. I saw Umpanu emerge from his house looking serious. The two stretchers were lowered onto the ground. Umpanu examined each wounded man in turn, then motioned for one of them to be taken to one of the huts. I soon heard moans and muffled screams.

Later Yaku told me that one warrior had been killed by an arrow to the chest. Another had had a spear thrust into his stomach. He was expected to live, but they wouldn't be certain for several weeks. The third man had received an arrow to his thigh. He would recover. I was told that the Suamu had also suffered casualties, including two killed. I find the whole thing fascinating and repulsive. I'm appalled by the behaviour of men, and I'm disgusted with myself that I also find it heroic and exciting.

Now Yaku tells me there will be a big feast, partly to honour the dead and the wounded, but also as a celebration of the battle itself, even though it was inconclusive. An intriguing part of the ceremony will be the two lots of warriors assembling on the boundary and facing each other across no man's land before the feast starts. Both sides will be armed and there will be much shouting and taunting, but there will be no fighting. Yaku says that each tribe will be displaying its honour of its own dead to the other. That's freaky. I'd half-decided that I would bunk off in order to watch, but Yaku's told me I'm needed to help prepare the feast. Also she's told me that Ekapamne is going to make me look very special.

. . . .

The men departed for their dissing ceremony, while we women started preparing the feast. A freakishly long sausage of a fruit, bright red and, big yikes, what were those? We were expected to fucking eat them? Ekapamne explained to me, partly using a few words I understood and partly by gestures, that the sago palm is very productive. They fell the trees and leave them to rot on the ground for a year. When they've gone all mushy, they split them open to find they're riddled with plump beetles and their even plumper grubs. I'd decided I would opt out from eating those, but then I found out that a Gucci dish I was about to help prepare consisted of a paste made of various green leaves and, hellishit, all those beetles and maggots mixed in. Yuck.

The women who knew how had been heating rocks to such a high temperature that a couple exploded, making me squawk, not the way a Walukek lady should behave. Others had created a huge bed of various kinds of leaves, hollowed in the middle. The men, who'd returned from their posturing, started to work on two piggies. Each was held by its ears and its hind legs. A third man then shot an arrow into the poor porker's chest. The first died quickly, but the other wriggled free and ran around squealing and pumping blood before it dropped down dead.

A couple of women started preparing the red sausage fruit. I didn't see much of what they were doing, because I was put onto the team to prepare what in the end would turn out to be the main vegetable dish. We made a concoction of ground sago powder, a sprinkle of some orange dusty stuff, many different sorts of leaves and herbs and - I knew it was coming - the beetles and grubs. All this lot was compressed, wrapped, and tightly bound in what looked like banana leaves, ready for the fire.

When the stones were hot enough, three of the women started putting them onto the cooking fire using long wooden tongs. One used her fingers, picking them up and throwing them all in one motion. I tried to do it, but screeched and dropped the rock onto my toes. I instantly had a sizzling hand and a bruised foot. I let rip with my fruitiest English swearwords while I hopped around, shaking my blistering hand. Too many of them found it funny. Yaku put some ointment onto it, which soothed it a bit, although it still throbbed. Meanwhile, the men were putting the joints of meat onto the fire. The women added the veg: taro, sweet potato, and my concoction. All the food was layered between wet leaves, then finally the whole pile was bound with thick vines, which I think are called lianas in some parts of the world.

We all went to our separate quarters to put on our bling, or in my case have it put on for me. Ekapamne made me wait while she got herself ready, assisted by one of her mates. When she emerged, she looked so spicy that I fancied her. Then she started on me. It was like being with Lily before the May Ball at Cambridge.

She used a palette of pastes of various colours, from orange to pure white and green. She worked on my face using a selection of wooden knives and spikes, some of them sharp, so I had to keep very still. Her fingers moving across my skin gave me goosebumps. When she'd finished, she sewed shells, bones, and I think somebody's teeth, onto my bib and skirt. She stood back and admired me from all angles, making a few adjustments where necessary. I was then crowned with a cap of red, blue, black, and green feathers. Yaku came up to me with her rusty mirror. I gasped and then couldn't help calling out,

'Fuck me real, that's so cool,' when I saw what I looked like. What Ekapamne had done was to make my face look beautiful. Yes, I said beautiful. I was so exquisitely made up that my ugliest features had become a logical part of my appearance. I looked feminine, exotic, tribal, and fierce. I tried to hug Ekapamne but she backed away laughing and I realised I would have ruined both our get-ups.

The other women had waited until we were all ready. We walked out towards the fire, admiring one another, then suddenly there was a hush. Out strutted the men, all proud and haughty, but it was the warriors who were the most magnificently shit-scary. Their eyes had been made up to look as terrible as one could possibly imagine with what looked like orange and black paint. Grease, probably pig fat, had been rubbed into their bodies, so that they shone like polished wood. Thin curved boar tusks sprouted from many of their noses. I wanted to stare at them and then look away, appalled by their frightfulness. Their heads were covered with so many bright colours that I guessed they were from birds of paradise which Penelope had told us about on the ship. What was freaky was that the men and women stared at each other with no acknowledgement. But I think the men were really inviting us to admire them, as if to say, 'Look at me and surrender to my awesome power.'

The two groups then went about their separate duties. The women broke up the fire, using the same tongs as before to remove the rocks. The smell wafting out made me salivate. I kept well clear this time. Then they all went rummaging to remove the veggie products, the taro and sweet potatoes, and the concoction I'd helped make. When they'd stood back, a few of the men removed the joints of pork and got to work breaking them up into portions. As everything was steaming hot, I thought they must have fingers made of leather.

A woman was unwrapping a bundle which I thought was the one I'd created. All the leaves had dissolved and the paste had become gooey, so that the result was a sort of moist bready dough, bright green, not what I'd expected.

The way the meal was served and eaten wasn't what I'd expected either. We all took stiff broad leaves which served as plates. A man doled out pieces of pork according to our status. I got one small chunk of meat and a tiny bit of skin. Then we walked over to two of the women, one of whom gave us a piece of sweet potato and a slice of taro. The other handed out portions of the doughy dish which had been my contribution. Then instead of eating communally, we all went to our separate huts and ate in groups of three or four. I have to say that the food was utterly yummy. The pork was succulent, complemented by the root vegetables, and the green pizza was a mixture of exotic flavours. I could see a grub and two beetles in mine, but I didn't care, so I devoured them as an essential part of the whole. When we'd finished, one of the women came round with little slices of sweet potato with a red sauce, which I guessed had been prepared from the huge sausage fruit. It too was delicious, the sourness and slight bitterness offset by the sweetness of the potato.

I wondered what would happen next, but it seemed it was siesta time. I didn't dare lie down in case I damaged my finery. I half-dozed for an hour or two, thinking of my parents and few friends back home. The long vac would soon be over. I wondered if Lily and the others were thinking of me and concluded that they would have forgotten. It didn't worry me; I was enjoying myself too much.

Just as it was getting dark, a succession of low whistles stirred us from our rest. Ekapamne stood up, stretched elegantly, smiled, and left the hut. I followed her. The men were gathering on one side of the communal patch and the women on the other. For the next three hours they paraded in succession. They never danced together. The men had just started when I noticed something spooky. The dead warrior had been propped up and was "watching" the performance, or rather a point somewhere above the dancers, with a sort of puzzled look. On his left, one of the wounded men was staring sadly as though he was taking his last look at the world. Every now and then the warriors would turn towards them and deliver a long shivering motion and a howl, I guessed as a mark of respect. Their singing was utterly tuneless, and their dancing little more than stomping to the rhythm of a small band of musicians who deserved better from their dancers. There were two bongos and a huge lateral tree trunk which was hammered in different parts to produce something approaching musical notes. Now and then three or four of the warriors would move out from the line and make various motions with their spears. I assumed they were telling some sort of story.

Now it was the women's turn. I held back, but Yaku beckoned me to join in. I felt exactly like when I'd been at the May Ball, awkward and shy. I watched the line of women carefully before attempting any movement myself. Ekapamne pulled me into the line. They strutted in unison, lolled their heads in a trance-like motion, and waggled their hips so that their skirts rustled and shivered. At first my moves imitated theirs. After some time, my inhibitions loosened, so I started juicing up my own thing. I forgot my duty to contribute to the communal performance. So I let rip, and that was when I committed my oh-my-cringe. I started doing what they must have taken as an erotic dance aimed directly at Ekapamne, because she pirouetted away, and the other women stopped dancing and returned to their positions facing the men. I felt a fool and wanted to run away, but I knew that would cause even more offence. So I retreated behind the others, my cheeks burning and my heart hammering. I wanted it all to end.

It went on for two more hours with not much variation, except that the men paid more attention to the dead body as the night wore on. The wounded man had disappeared. My impression of the whole evening was that the dress and make-up were sophisticated and exotic, the dancing not.

I'm loving it here. Their way of life fascinates me. I'm especially drawn to Ekapamne. She's fun and I find her sexy. But I realise I can't stay here. That crazy idea of this being my gap year isn't on. I would vegetate and I need the stimulus of intellectual challenge. Not having the internet, not even having a phone or a means of charging one, not being able to look again at my response to Dollen's Theory of Consequential Lensing or my PhD proposal, it's driving me wild. I have to get back to those things.

I know I look ghastly. Here they seem to accept me as I am. Back home, I can imagine how people will react. It will be horrible for the rest of my life. I will never get used to it. Face to face relationships have always scared the shit out of me and now the very word face disgusts me. But my brain's intact and my ability to network internationally will still be there. I have to do it.

I waited until I was alone with Yaku and Umpanu. But when I tried to tell them what I wanted, I went into my silent mode.

Umpanu seemed to know what I was going to say. 'You cannot stay here. I have cured you.'

I burst into tears. Yaku laid a hand on my arm and I fell onto her, sobbing. Umpanu gave me some time, and then told me what he planned.

'A man with a boat brought you to me. He saved your life. He can take you back to where the big ship comes.'

Having wanted that, I now became terrified. I hadn't got any money, or a phone, or a passport. I didn't even know exactly where I was. 'So,' I howled, 'what will happen to me then? I can't even, I can't even...' I couldn't get the words out. But I could say this. 'I love you.'

He looked embarrassed but said nothing more. It seems that his plan for me hasn't got beyond that small island where big ships dock occasionally. I remembered its name, Sundabang. It's where I left the cruise ship, apparently. I haven't been given a date for my departure, just a hint that it should be soon.

....

Two days later, I was working in the fields as usual with some of the women when something strange happened. One of them let out a sort of bark. The others froze and then straightened. They were staring towards the edge of the forest. They remained motionless and silent for some time. I couldn't see anything. They seemed reluctant to return to their work and then an argument started. After several minutes, a decision seemed to have been reached, because they all began to move off, back in the direction of the village. That was odd because we'd only been there for a little over half an hour. I tried to ask Ekapamne what was happening, but she pretended not to understand me. I asked Yaku about it that evening.

'They are nervous because they have seen some men watching them. They think they may be Suamu warriors.'

'Can some of the men not come to guard us?'

Yaku seemed to think the suggestion absurd. 'They will not come.'

I wasn't sure whether that meant that Walukek men wouldn't guard us, or whether Yaku was indicating that the Suamu warriors wouldn't approach closer.

I might have thought about it a bit more, except that I'd developed a mild fever. Umpanu treated me with some potion, and I soon started to recover. Yaku insisted that I rest for three more days in isolation. I was fucking bored. I tried to tackle Dollen's Theory of Consequential Lensing, which was difficult in my head, but not impossible. I fretted that I couldn't see where I might have gone wrong. I gained little comfort from thinking that perhaps I hadn't.

....

I couldn't sleep. Pressing myself up off the floor, I tiptoed past the slumbering bodies, and ducked through the entrance. The air bore a heady concoction of earthy aromas too subtle for individual identification.

A slight breeze drifting through the trees. Drawn to the edge of the forest as though sleepwalking. So many leaves fluttering across the surface of the full moon, preventing light from reaching the forest floor. Looking up, swaying, mesmerised by moonbeams. So beautiful, so familiar, but here so alien. That same moon shining down into college quad a few hours ago will do so again tonight. An owl hooting away to my left, indifferent and remote.

I'm here and yet not here. There is a rustling through the undergrowth ahead of me. I ought to care what it is, but I don't. What if I do have a great understanding of quantum chromodynamics? Oh Lily, I'm so lonely. What is happening to me?

PART V

I'm still trembling. I thought I was going to be killed this morning and I still may be. I'm sweating and yet I'm shivering. I can't bring my breathing under control. I feel dizzy and unreal, but at least I've stopped retching. It's fully dark and I can no longer see the walls of this house they've put me in. The rain is making a hissing sound on the thatch. The couch I'm lying on isn't uncomfortable and the temperature's normal. That's the air. My body temperature's off the scale. I ought to sleep, but I can't stop gulping and quaking.

I'm in delayed shock, I know I am, delayed because for much of the day I fought back. I wasn't going to give the fuckers the pleasure of seeing me break. So until I was locked away in this house, I asserted myself and showed no weakness. But once the pressure was off and I was alone, I deflated like a farting balloon.

I don't want to think about what happened today, but I can't help it. I'm missing Ekapamne and remembering her has set me off sobbing again. She's safe, I think she is. When the warriors tried to isolate me from the other women, Ekapamne refused to leave me. For half a minute we stood shoulder to shoulder futilely jabbing the sharpened ends of our wooden mattocks towards their weapons, which were four times as long as ours. Then one of the men took a firm swipe with the side of his spear. Ekapamne stumbled, and two of the others dived in between us, so we were finally parted. I screamed at her to run. The other Walukek women had held back, but now it was obvious that it was me they were after and there was nothing they could do to save me. So they all started running back towards the village and I don't blame them.

I wasn't going to give in easily. There aren't many advantages of having a face like a demented banshee, but one of them is that if I'm going to look frightful, I might as well act like it. So instead of cowering, I darted towards each of them in turn, hissing, snarling, and using the foulest vernacular English I could think of. Even so, I hadn't expected the reaction I got. They all jumped back as though I was carrying a nuclear bomb. So then I thought, sheesh, I seem to have the upper hand, at least for now, so I might as well play badass. I went rigid and gave each of them in turn my cold stare, the one I use on all my enemies: Josh, Bruce, and Professor Coulter. It looked as though they were shitting themselves. They eyed each other nervously, so I planted my feet apart, put my hands on my hips, and smiled triumphantly at them, even though I didn't feel like it. They began jabbering at each other in a language I didn't understand.

Then I thought of something even better. I started to do the *haka* like the good Maori my mother thinks I am. So I roared and went hoo-hoo-hoo and shivered my fingers. I slapped my elbows and thighs, not very successfully because of my tree bark skirt. I stuck my tongue out, planted my feet apart, and stamped to the rhythm of my bellowing.

I'd been acting out so much drama that I hadn't noticed what the men were doing. When I'd finished rolling my eyes, I focussed on them. They were still surrounding me but had dropped back in a sort of open ring, like a horseshoe. So I simply walked into the gap, intending to turn, once outside, and run back to my village. But they wouldn't let me. Still keeping their distance, but with their spears pointing at me, they drove me in the direction they wanted me to go.

There was nothing I could do to prevent it. Up to now, I'd been high on anger and adrenaline. Now the inevitability of realising I'd been captured and was being forced away robbed me of all hope that I could resist. Fear took over, with one terror dominating all others: gang rape.

I was marched through the dripping forest for, I don't know, something like a couple of hours, until my captors started calling out with shrill bell-like tones which seemed to knock back from the trees. It was some time before I realised that the echoes were in fact answering calls from up ahead.

'Weh-eh, weh-oh, kok kok, e-kok weh-eh.'

We entered what I now realised must have been a Suamu village. Although the cleared area in front of the huts was larger than the Walukeks', the houses themselves blended more closely into the trees. The whole place seemed dark, secretive, and sinister. Mist and smoke hung menacingly in the trees. Water dripped from the leaves. Men and women, but no children, were emerging through the gloom as though they'd been standing there all along. Were their stares hostile or fearful? I waved to them. No one waved back, but one of the women turned and ran back through her doorway.

An elderly woman came up to us. Her face was painted with yellow and white markings which made her look so frightful that it brought back a childhood nightmare I used to have of being tormented by a witch. She said a few words I couldn't understand. The men moved me on again. They seemed to be ushering me out of the village, until they swung right and drove me towards a hut at the edge of the settlement. Another woman, less exotically dressed, gave me an elaborate salute and indicated that I should enter. Too tired, wet, and frightened to do anything else, I ducked through the small doorway. So here I am, a prisoner of a fierce and hostile tribe, awaiting my fate.

....

I've been here for three whole days. I can tell it's morning because even this enclosed hut lets in a few chinks of light. And I can hear that bird again. Its first few notes rise and then tip over into a tumbling, bell-like cascade. I've been fed, quite well in fact, although my appetite's still poor. Continual fear has deadened me, fear of why I'm here and what they intend to do to me. I've got no saliva, my mouth is dry, and it feels as though I've got something solid stuck in my throat.

A woman comes in each morning. After she's done a bow and a series of flamboyant gestures towards me with her hands, I'm invited to wash myself with a gourd full of water and some grease, which is quite a good substitute for soap. When I want to relieve myself, I call out and the same woman enters. I know I wouldn't be able to overpower her, because every time she comes in, a man carrying a spear pokes his nose in behind her. Relieving myself in the forest with a warrior ogling me and carrying a dirty great spike in his hand is as hard as it sounds. The stuff takes ages to come.

This morning, after I'd been escorted to and from my watched-upon poo and had lathered, rinsed, and dried, I resigned myself to another tedious day in the dark. But then two women came in. They were quite old, severe, but respectful. Having saluted me elaborately, they carefully put their hands on my shoulders and waist and very slowly started to undress me, cooing all the time. My first instinct was to flap and scream at them, but this time I decided I was going to remain silent, lie back, relax, and think of Einstein. Whatever the police say when making an arrest seemed appropriate. "You do not have to say anything, but anything you do say may be given in evidence against you." That's my right enshrined in Suamu law, the right to remain silent. Says no one.

I was given a new skirt made of dark brown rushes. They painted me all over with white dots, including my face. My hair was allowed to hang free. Apart from strings of brown and white shells and pieces of bone, which they carefully draped across my cleavage, that was it. Then I thought, shit, those don't look like pieces of bone, I think they're teeth, human teeth.

I had no way of knowing what my face looked like. One of the women had spent a long time decorating it, but whether she'd made the best of my scars, as Ekapamne had done, I couldn't tell. The other woman had left the hut. It seemed we were having to wait until we were summoned. It was only then that I realised, OMG, that my boobs were going to remain exposed. There's nothing wrong with them; they're firm and well-proportioned for my stature, but I don't make a habit of airing them in public. So, Athena, you'd better lie back and think of someone other than Einstein.

The other woman returned and repeated the same elaborate greeting. They both made it clear that it was time to go.

I was led into the middle of the village. Well over a hundred people were standing around the edge of the central clearing. I knew instantly from my knowledge of the Walukek and from Penelope's lecture on the ship that they were dressed in their ceremonial bling. And I also realised there were too many for them all to be inhabitants of this village. Others must have been bussed in, metaphorically speaking. They'd set up a sort of hissing sound like wind in dry grass. If the intention was to intimidate me, it was working. I was trying to control my shakes. Don't let them see your fear, I told myself. Ahead of me, I could see a large pile of rushes with curved bark on top. A long stone like a petrified tree trunk lay in front of it. That was going to be where they would perform some barbaric ritual act on me: rape, genital mutilation, execution. Don't let them see your fear. Keep saying it, don't let them see your fear.

I was led up to the pile of rushes and invited to sit down. These people gazing and hissing at me might have thought that it was some type of throne, but to me it looked like a giant version of the beanbag on which Teddy and I had lain at the May Ball. Some comfort that was. I'd been shitting myself there too. I was about to lower myself onto the curved bark, which was clearly a seat, when I thought, fuck no, I'll be doing what they want me to do. Seize the initiative, you dumb bag. So I stayed standing and flicked away the two women who'd been escorting me. I held my hands out from my sides, palms facing forward. Making what I hoped was the best use of my ghastly face, I uttered just one sharp sound. 'Huh.' The hissing stopped.

Still keeping my arms out, I surveyed my audience. My eyes were drawn first to a man who looked as though he was about to be filmed on a Hollywood set. His face was covered in white dots of varying sizes. His eyes were surrounded by a sort of eggy yellow and he seemed to have two levels of hair. The upper, which must have been a wig, was jet black, exploding in all directions. Below that a white band, looking as though it was made of teeth, topped a thick ochre fringe of frizzy hair, possibly his own. But it was his nose which made him look, like, eye-poppingly scary. Two thin white bones curved up on either side from his nostrils to his temples. He had large eyes with dilated pupils and a wolfish expression. It took an effort to move my eyes away from his face and examine the rest of his body. His torso and arms were naked, except that they weren't, because less than half of his skin was visible, the rest being covered with armlets, tattoos, and strings of teeth, bones, and shit knows what else. He wore a brief bark-cloth skirt, below which his muscular legs were bare, though heavily decorated.

On either side of him, four other men, only slightly less exotically adorned, were also staring at me. My eyes were just about to leave them when I noticed, jeez, those impressive looking pecs were actually boobs, and I was looking at women. Like, this was so not like the Walukek village, where the women may dress up, but they sure as eggs don't mix with the men and flash their tits. I had to take my eyes off them. I needed to take control. Don't let them see your fear.

I decided to get spunky again. Still refusing to sit down, I roared the only thing I could think of, which was the first law of thermodynamics. That didn't work very well. It's impossible to shout out the word "equilibrium" and make it sound angry. Nobody moved, nobody said anything, they all just stared at me. The words were too dry to convey drama and fury. So I tried Queen Elizabeth's speech at Tilbury.

'I know I have the body of a weak and feeble woman. Huh? But I have the heart and strength of a king. Votes for women. Deeds not words. Huh?'

They seemed enthralled so I had to keep going. I've never really been into Shakespeare, but I remembered bits of *King Lear* from my schooldays.

'Blow winds and crack your cheeks. Rage, blow, you cataracts and hurricanoes. Huh?'

Still I held my audience. I must be a fucking actress, but I was running out of ideas. Don't give up, I told myself; you're fighting for your life. I remembered watching a video of Adolf Hitler giving a speech. I don't speak German, so I had to make up the words, but I could recall his gestures. I used a gradually rising pitch and intensity, starting off pointing my hands towards my mouth as though drawing the words out. I finally flung my right arm out and shouted *'Sieg Heil!'*. I paused and turned my nightmarish face on to each group of my audience in turn. That did produce a reaction. The man in the centre clenched his fists and then flung his right arm out in a gesture that mirrored mine. What the fuck did that mean? Was it a sign of acknowledgement, a mutual exchange of body language? Had *Mein Fuehrer* been accepted into the tribe?

No, he hadn't. Two warriors and two of the scary women were advancing towards me.

I was still terrified of ceding the initiative. I thought of moving on to Planck's Constant but decided the words weren't suitable for conveying anger either. So I shouted out, 'You cannot shake hands with a clenched fist. Huh?'

The advancing warriors and women had paused fifteen feet in front of me. My whole audience seemed agog, but I couldn't keep this up. I was no longer lost in my performance. Reality was taking over. I needed to know what the shit was happening and, more importantly, what was going to happen. So I ended my act by strutting around clapping my hands above my head. Finally I did a curtsey in front of the women, hoping that this last flourish looked impressive in my grass skirt. I stayed crumpled with one knee bent, hands held together in the *namaste* position, head bowed like I'd seen ballerinas do at the end of a performance. I hoped it looked graceful and submissive. I thought it best to pass the initiative back to the Suamu now. I unfolded myself and stepped back onto the seat which they'd wanted me to use at the beginning. I had no more ideas of what to do.

Now that I'd become passive, it seemed that everyone had a script except me. Two warriors took up their positions on either side of my throne. Three younger women now appeared carrying baskets made of woven bark. The first contained brightly coloured flowers and feathers. One of those huge red fruits shaped like a sausage, which I'd seen at the Walukek feast, had been laid in the other. But it was the contents of the third which made me give one of those single jerks which I sometimes get as I'm going off to sleep. My lower jaw started involuntarily chattering. There, being reverently placed on the altar, were a stone axe and a sharpened bamboo stick.

One of the older women held out her arms and made a gesture that I was to rise. She turned to each of the separate groups, both men and women, and kinda blessed them, like *Il Papa* himself. They all started wailing, the sound steadily rising in intensity. Their voices started to quaver and the effect was chilling. Had I made a huge mistake by ending up being submissive? Was I going to be led to that stone in front of me? Human sacrifice? Gang rape? Mutilation? I could already imagine my blood trickling down the altar and the pain of that stone axe and sharpened stick. The wailing was rising in pitch. A climax was coming, I knew it. I was totally bricking it. It had all been leading up to this. To what? To me.

I fainted.

PART VI

My name is Rachel Atkinson, Dr Rachel Atkinson, MBE. I'm an anthropologist, specialising in remote tribes of Papua New Guinea, mainly those of West Papua. I have also carried out research in the nearby Banda and Maluku archipelagos. I expect you have seen me on television. I present, produce, and occasionally direct documentaries. I have contacts high up in the BBC and other television networks, and in several leading universities.

This year I'm concentrating my research on the Suamu and Walukek tribes of West Papua. There are many reasons why I'm attracted to them. They are still living in the stone age, and although they practise some agriculture, the Walukek more than the Suamu, part of their life is spent as hunter gatherers. But what is astonishing, and possibly unique in Papua New Guinea, is their relationship with each other. The Suamu and Walukek fight one another regularly, brutally, and without warning, but between them they have managed to control and avoid the corruption of warfare which has blighted most of the rest of the island. The elders of the two tribes have agreed a code of conduct which has largely been adhered to. It is as though the Suamu and Walukek have drawn up their own Geneva Convention.

The use of firearms and machetes has been totally banned by both sides for the past ten years or so. The weapons used are bows, arrows, and spears, as they were in previous centuries. Most importantly, and this is where the uniqueness comes in, the elders have managed to control their youths. In so many other tribes, nearly all in fact, attacks by young men take place unscheduled, using guns and bombs, so that people are massacred and burned to death in their houses at night.

Even so, it's far from idyllic between the Suamu and Walukek. Warriors get killed and maimed in these battles. More insidiously, kidnapping takes place, although this is sometimes resolved by payment of ransoms, which usually means pigs. Where the victim is a man, he will often be repatriated via prisoner swaps. But women are not so often returned. When a woman is kidnapped, a battle may be fought in revenge, but that does not always succeed in the recovery of the unfortunate female. And it is an ugly part of this culture that rape is practised, sometimes openly in the fields and cloud forest.

The Suamu are unusual in another way too. Nearly all the tribes of Papua New Guinea are patriarchal. They're also patrilineal, meaning that wealth passes through the male line. Not so the Suamu, who are matrilineal. Land is owned by and inherited by the women. But that doesn't mean that the Suamu are matriarchal. It's fascinating. I'm a long way from getting to understand it fully, and that's one of the main reasons why I'm going to visit them. Put very crudely, the women are responsible for much, but not all, of the decision making within the village. The men are totally responsible outside; one could call that foreign policy, which includes when to go to war and when to negotiate with the Walukek. The women have no say in that.

I'm not taking a camera crew with me this time. I'm going there for research, not to make a documentary. That may come later. I'll be accompanied by a female translator, Bili. She's a Suamu, but knows the Walukek and is fluent in both languages. All I'll take is a single change of clothes, wash things, medication, sanitary towels, a small head rest, a head torch, and my tablet and phone. The absence of electricity is a problem, as it can be cloudy for weeks at a time, so solar power isn't always reliable. There are no lights at night other than fires, not even candles. I'm taking a hand-cranked charger as the ultimate backup. I'll visit the Suamu first and then I'll move on to the Walukek.

I'm hoping we'll be housed in an *ebeai*, that's a communal house for women in a *sili*, a compound within the village. We'll be living right amongst the Suamu women and Bili can listen in on their conversations. That way she can pass on the gossip to me. One learns more from eavesdropping than from formal interviews.

But there is a disadvantage of living in an *ebeai*. Fires burn in every house. They are the sole means of light as well as heat. The huts have no chimneys, so the smoke builds up inside until it eventually finds its way through the thatch, which I have been warned is particularly thick on Suamu houses. Lung disease is a major reason why Papuan tribespeople have such short lives. I'm used to taking calculated risks: malaria, encephalitis, dengue fever, you name it, and remember I will be several days from the nearest hospital. But those are diseases which one either catches or one does not, and I can take measures to minimise the risks. Not so smoke inhalation, which is unavoidable and cumulative the longer one remains in an *ebeai*. For that reason, I will not stay with the Suamu and the Walukek for more than a month each.

....

The first leg of my journey, to Jakarta, was completed on time. Being in business class, I slept well on the plane. I had a meeting with the Minister of Home Affairs and the Minister responsible for indigenous tribes, who has such a long title that even I have difficulty remembering it. I'm a trustee of the charity Mined Out, and I also have contacts high up in Amnesty International. Small-scale illegal gold mining has been taking place on the northern border of the Suamu's territory for several years. I'd got to hear that a local company, funded by a South

African conglomerate, has been lobbying for a contract to carry out large-scale mining which would encroach well within the Suamu border. It was obvious that there was corruption at a regional level, but I wasn't sure how things stood with the government in Jakarta. I needn't have worried. The ministers not only told me that the mining concession would not be granted, they also said that the illegal miners were being thrown off the land as we were speaking. I'd got what I wanted, so I had some good news to bring to the Suamu.

My next flight was late, so that I missed my connection to a third. I took to Bili the moment we shook hands. She's short with plump cheeks and a willing smile. The bus was dirty and smelly, so the jeep ride, although bumpy, came as a relief. Eventually we could be transported no further, so we heaved our rucksacks onto our backs and trekked. There was a brief shower early on, but for most of the walk it was misty but dry.

I always feel a thrill when I enter a Papuan settlement, tempered by nervousness at what sort of reception I might get. This time, I hoped that the good news I was bringing would make the Suamu welcome my presence, not just tolerate it.

The village was surrounded by fortifications of earth banks, piles of brushwood, and stakes pointing upwards and outwards, always a sign of hostilities with neighbouring tribes. The houses seemed rather forbidding, being buried under a smothering mountain of thatch.

It was interesting that a woman came out to greet us rather than a man. We were ushered into one of the *silis*. The inhabitants melted into their huts, the women to their *ebeais* and the men to their *pilais*. Another woman brought us kava to drink. There being no furniture, which is normal in a Papuan *sili*, we squatted. I'm used to it.

Three people entered the *sili*, a man and two women, none of them young. They were richly adorned and decorated, I guessed due to their status rather than the occasion. They greeted us formally but without warmth. The women were more severe than the man. I gave them the gifts I had brought, a carved wooden bowl and four elaborately woven bilum bags.

My opening gambit, which Bili translated, is always the same. 'I am honoured to be here, and I thank you for allowing me to visit you.'

The man inclined his head.

'I do not wish to intrude on your way of life in any way. I am here to respect everything you do and to take part in whatever way you wish.'

Papuan tribes never ask how one's journey has been or anything about one's own life. Any explanation would be meaningless to them in any case. They have little comprehension of the world beyond their territory. That is why they have retained their culture. I am here to study them, not the other way round.

'I have been told that illegal gold mining has been taking place at the northern end of your territory.'

The man looked uneasy. 'There is fighting there.'

'Bili, ask them who is fighting whom.'

'The gold diggers are attacking the soldiers.'

That sounded unlikely.

A delicious meal was brought to us on bark plates. I recognised taro, sago, and an especially tasty mash made from green leaves and herbs. I needed more protein than they did. There were freshwater crayfish in the streams. Bili would see to it.

'I have come from meeting important men in the government.' They wouldn't know much about what went on in Jakarta, but I was confident they would understand the word "government". The man looked expectant, the women neutral, as though they hadn't understood.

'There will be no more gold mining on your land.'

The man started talking rapidly to the two women. Bili made no attempt to translate but turned to me when they'd finished. 'He says that the fighting stopped three days ago and the men have gone. He says that what you have said is good.'

I bowed my head, accepting his implied gratitude.

....

It's my third day here. Bili and I have settled in to our *ebeai*. We share it with three other women, all married. It's remarkable how quickly they've accepted our presence. Their husbands live in a separate *pilai*. There are three *ebeais* and three *pilais* within this *sili*, which also contains two other huts, one for cooking and washing, and the other for meeting. Ours is quite a small *sili*. It seems there are eight *silis* in this village. It's normal to find the men and women sleeping separately. I'll be interested to discover what the arrangements are for sexual intercourse. It will need patience and tact. I have both.

Our presence here seems to have been accepted remarkably quickly. Only the odd person stares at us, and then only briefly. The men ignore us more than the women. Bili and I have been assigned one woman from our *ebeai* called Venakli. Her job is to show us what to do and answer any questions. I've warned Bili that we must make sure that not everything is channelled through Venakli. I've found in the past that guides are often instructed to paint a rosy picture and try to prevent me from finding out the less pleasant truths. If that is Venakli's brief, it failed spectacularly this afternoon. I'm not easily shocked, but I have to admit that I got quite a scare.

Venakli had taken us to see the sacred stones, which are the tribal totems. We admired them without touching them. She then took us half a mile or so to see the mummies. These are the shrunken remains of Suamu ancestors, which stand propped up against a bank. Most people might find them spooky, but I'm used to that sort of thing. Bili and I squatted before them to pay our respects. Leathery skeletons leered back at us from another time.

That wasn't the shock, which came after we'd returned. We were bending over a large stone near the centre of the village communal area, wondering what it was used for. It was just starting to get dark. I was in mid-conversation with Bili when I became aware of a presence close by. I straightened and turned to see a horrific looking creature staring at me. With the image of the mummies still in my head, I couldn't at first grasp that this apparition was actually alive. It took me several seconds more to realise that it was a young woman, clearly a Suamu girl, who'd been horribly mutilated, either intentionally or accidentally. It wasn't just that she looked repulsive, it was that she was staring at me, not at Bili but at me, with a look so malevolent that I hate to admit it, I was terrified. It wasn't just her expression, it was the way that, over a period of a couple of minutes, she didn't seem to move a muscle. I pulled myself together. Dr Atkinson, I told myself, act professionally. I started to move towards her. She took several steps swiftly back and then glided towards the edge of the forest. I speculated wildly. Perhaps she wasn't a member of the village? She was a wanderer, an outcast? She was one of the spirits which these tribes so strongly believe exist? Don't be ridiculous! That I was thinking these things is a measure of how strongly I'd been jolted. I asked Bili if she knew anything, but she shook her head vigorously. Bili looked as shaken as I was.

. . . .

Although I'm still missing Ekapamne, in many ways I've got it better than when I was with the Walukek. I don't know how long I've been here because this time I haven't been keeping a record. It must be at least a month. I'm given good food by two ladies-in-waiting. If I point to the stuff I like and give the thumbs up, they seem to understand and give me more. I'm treated respectfully, although I'm still accompanied by a voyeur with a poker when I go for a poop in the forest.

Suamu houses look different from the Walukeks', which are on stilts. These rest straight onto the ground. The top-heavy thatch comes right down over the bamboo and wooden uprights, so that only a metre or so of the walls is visible. They look suppressed, as though both houses and their inhabitants are being suffocated. Another thing I've noticed from my early morning crap forays is how the village is fortified by a defensive ring of earth banks, heaped up brushwood, and sharpened stakes driven into the ground.

But I am safe and so far haven't been molested or dissed. I thought I was going to die on that first night when I came here. Then three days later there was that weird ceremony in front of that stone altar, when I was shitting myself wondering if I was going to be gang raped, have my bits cut off and eaten, or sacrificed to the spirits of the forest. None of those happened. After I'd recovered from my faint, a pig was dragged in front of me and a bow and arrow held aloft. For one shitty moment I thought that I was being asked to slaughter it myself, then realised that perhaps I ought to bless it. I made the sign of the cross and said in my clearest voice, *'In nomine Patris et Filii et Spiritus Sancti.'* That seemed to satisfy them because the man drew back his bow and shot the poor porker dead. I looked forward to the choicest cut and some piggy scratchings. And I got them. At the Walukeks' feast, I'd been given a measly lump of meat and a tiny flaccid piece of skin. Here, I'll swear I had the biggest and best portion.

It turned out that the stone axe was for cutting up the red sausage fruit, which was smeared all over my shoulders and boobs. The sharpened stick which had so frightened me had been used as a sort of bodkin to adorn me with the flowers and feathers. Before I knew it, I'd become a bird of paradise. Because, you see, I began to realise that, instead of being sacrificed, I was being worshipped.

After that, there was chanting and dancing. Everything seemed to be directed at me. I decided that if I joined in, it would diminish my status and reduce me to being one of them. Athena, you're a goddess, I told myself, act like one. I didn't make any more speeches, there didn't seem to be any point. I sat on the rush and bark throne for most of the time, but when someone came up to me, I blessed them.

I can go where I like. A warrior stands outside my house at night, but I'm sure that's to protect me, not restrain me. By day I wander where I please. One of my ladies-in-waiting accompanies me at a respectful distance wherever I go. Everywhere, people salute me with their palms pointing towards me. I'm not allowed to work. Each time I've seen one of the women cleaning a pan or sweeping the soil in front of a house and have tried to join in, I've been politely restrained, always with salutations before and after. I'm badly in need of exercise and would love to go for a run in the forest, but running would be undignified, especially with my swinging boobs. I must always remember that I'm Athena.

I've picked up a few snippets of the Suamu language. There's one particular word which sounds like golgola. They were chanting it monotonously at the ceremony, but I've heard it at other times too, directed at me. A few people use the odd word of Walukek, not whole sentences, but words which I recognise. I asked a young man in Walukek whether I might walk in the forest. He looked terrified, saluted me elaborately, backed away, and ran off into one of the other compounds. He came back with one of the lady elders. So now I'm allowed to go for walks, accompanied by a warrior with bow and arrows and one of my ladies-in-waiting. But only in certain directions. If I try to walk towards the Walukek village or to the south, they politely turn me back. I could use my status to defy them, but I'm there for the exercise, not to cause trouble.

I got a shock when I returned to the village today. I'd walked into the centre where I'd had my frightening ordeal a few weeks ago. Two women in western dress were examining the stone altar. The first was dark like me, but the other was a tall blonde of about forty. She turned round and seemed to jump with fright. Her face screwed up with a look of utter disgust. I was so angry that it took me some time to remember my disfigured face. I'm so used to being revered by the Suamu and tolerated by the Walukek that it's easy to forget how monstrous I look. For a couple of minutes, I couldn't move, and neither, it seemed, could she. Normally when I put on my frozen stare, it's for effect, but this time I was involuntarily rooted to the spot. Then I stepped back, turned round, and fled back to my hut, a lady-in-waiting in pursuit.

....

There are strange things going on in this village. Bili keeps apologising to me that this isn't normal and that she doesn't understand what's happening. I've told her to be patient and observe. That zombie-like creature seems to wander where she pleases, in and out of the *silis* at will. I've even seen her snooping into our own *ebeai*. She always seems to be followed by one or other of the women. She appears keen to avoid us, but when I do corner and step in front of her, she freezes. I try to look compassionately at her, but it's difficult when she pierces me with that malevolent stare.

....

Fucking tourists. I've taken an instant disliking to the tall one. She has high cheek bones, a straight nose, blue eyes, and a long bony figure. When I first had that confrontation with her, she looked at me with contempt, as though she had a bad smell under her nose. Now I wish she'd stop treating me as though I was some freak she wants to explore. She keeps trying to step in front of me. When she does so, I freeze. I'm being examined as though I'm a piece of meat that's gone off. I can see her nostrils flaring like she's a horse. The other one's small with a round face and low brow, which they all seem to have in this part of Indonesia.

This is getting more interesting by the minute. The men mostly ignore her, but the women seem to be treating her with respect and even reverence. They have a way of greeting her with their palms outstretched. But she doesn't seem to speak to anyone. I'm beginning to wonder whether her physical disability has made her mute.

....

Maybe I was wrong about the tourists. They've been here for four days, and no other outsiders have appeared. The blonde bitch seems to be taking notes. If she starts sketching me or taking pictures, I'll kill her. I think she's English. She's certainly speaking in English with a lah-di-dah accent. Although she disses me and I can't stand her, I wonder whether I should after all cultivate her. She might possibly be a means of escape. The longer I stay here, the more desperate I am to get back to Cambridge, Dollen, and networking. I'll try and listen in on them and see what I can pick up.

....

I've tried getting Bili to find out who she is and why they're treating her this way. All Bili's got from them is that she's not a Suamu and that they consider her presence a blessing. At first I thought that she looked like a local in every way. Her skin is exactly the right colour, as are her eyes and hair. All the tribes I've met around here have low brows. Hers are arched above her round eyes. If it wasn't for what's happened below, I'd say that her visual aspect is remarkably open.

....

I must be patient. I need to get close to that Karen and her gofer. If I can listen to why they're here and what they've heard about me, I might just be able to open up to them, but not before I know I can trust them. I've got a plan. There's a gap in a slat right by where they sleep. They go to rest there for an hour or so before my warrior comes to guard me in my hut. I won't be able to sit outside without my lady-in-waiting coming close, but I don't see that as a problem. I'll just lounge there chewing the cud and wait for them to start talking. As the two bitches know that the Suamu women can't understand a word of what they're saying in English, there'll be no reason for them to be discreet. And with luck they won't know I'm listening.

....

I asked if we could interview the most senior women tomorrow. Bili says they've agreed. I'll ask them directly who the girl is and what she's doing here. I'm not sure about Bili. I have a feeling she knows more than she's prepared to tell me.

....

That was so-o frustrating. I could hear what they were saying, but only just. Heavy rain hammering onto leaves and hissing in the thatch didn't help, and every now and then thunderclaps eliminated all other sounds. I didn't find out much about what they're doing here and even less about why the Suamu captured me and seem to worship me. What I did find out made me want to shout out, 'Cunt!', not just because the blonde bitch was talking crap, but also because she dissed me, the ignorant cow. This is what I heard.

"She's clearly mentally retarded. She must be, with that vacant look and the fact that she can't speak except for a few mumbled noises, and those not very often."

"Her face is not nice."

"No, and the way she just stands there without moving, looking as though she wants to cry, makes me think she's mentally disabled. What I can't understand is why they seem to think she's so wonderful, powerful even."

I'll have you know, I muttered to myself, that I'm Athena, a brilliant scientist and mathematician, worshipped by Professor Kovacs, sought by Professor Dollen, and feared by Professor Coulter.

....

At last I know a bit about the girl. She's not a Suamu or even a Walukek. They say she comes from far away. They call her Golgola and say she's very special. Her presence, they say, is a blessing to the tribe, but also a curse. I got the impression that it could be disastrous for them if they were to upset her.

While the two women were having some kind of meeting with the female elders in one of the other compounds, I snuck into their hut and started going through their things. My lady-in-waiting remained outside.

Her name is Dr Rachel Atkinson, MBE. What kind of a bumpiece puts her poncey title, no doubt earned by licking several arses, onto her luggage label? If I do ever get to talk to her, I shall call her Ma'am with my best sneer. I tried booting up her tablet. It was password protected, but I did manage to find a paper stuck into her passport which gave the reason for her visit. She's here for a month doing a research project on the Suamu and then, OMG, she's going on to do the same with the Walukek. A month! So at least I can take my time and think carefully how to approach her, properly, I mean. I was tempted to take her passport as a bargaining chip. I may yet do so. The other female's Indonesian.

....

It came to me in a flash as I was getting off to sleep. I've little time for Anelise Scheldt. Her fieldwork is sloppy and her conclusions often bizarre. Anthropologists don't like to use the word "primitive", but Scheldt sprays it around carelessly. She even called the Tuli people "savages". Unforgiveable. But she's visited the Suamu twice and probably knows them better than anyone since Jameson in the eighties. It was the name Golgola that rang a bell. My battery's low and I need to conserve my tablet for my interviews. Even so, I just had to look up what Scheldt had written.

"There are many ghosts in the forest, in the villages, and even in the houses. Although some of the Suamu claim to glimpse them occasionally, few would deny that they've sensed them, and all believe in them. Most of these spirits are current, others in the past, meaning that they no longer have a presence. Either the Suamu's oral tradition has failed to go on recounting them so that they have been lost for ever, or they have been consciously assigned to history by the storytellers, departed but nevertheless believed to have existed. Many have been exorcised by rituals.

"These ghosts are either the spirits of dead ancestors or else of enemies killed in battle. That defines them as having lived in the past. So it is remarkable that the Suamu also recognise a powerful force who is yet to come. There has only been one other recorded case in Papua New Guinea of this belief in a messiah, recorded by Josephs in the Dara tribe in 1954. The Suamu's anticipated spirit is believed to be both terrible and a force for good, although when it appears, tradition has it that its benevolence will not be apparent. Its name is Golgola.

"There is much vagueness as to the details. There is even some doubt about whether Golgola will be male or female, although it is always referred to as "he". Most accounts agree that Golgola will be terrible to look at. Opinions differ as to how he should be treated, although the majority believe that he should be honoured and worshipped. A few

134

think he should be left to do whatever he has come to do. Some even go so far as to say that his appearance will be so frightful that merely looking at him will be fatal. Most spirits originate from within the forest, but a further variation is that Golgola will come from the sea. One thing all prophets agree on: his arrival will be a very great day for the tribe."

....

I don't know whether to be fascinated or terrified. This evening I was able to listen to more of the bitches' conversation.

'Her name is Golgola and they say that she's a spirit who has been long awaited.'

That name made me jump so much that I had to pull sharply back from my listening post. It's the name the Suamu have been calling me.

'How long has she been here?'

'They say a couple of moons.'

'Do you know where she has come from?'

I leaned in close to the gap in the slat to hear how the little dark one would reply. I was so close to them that I needed to be careful that they didn't hear me if I pressed too hard against the slat or if I darkened the room in the dying light.

'They say she came from over the sea.'

'The sea? The Suamu aren't near the sea. It's about eight hours' walk away, but that's through hostile territory, the Walukeks'. Did they say how she got here?'

'They did not want to answer that question.'

I just restrained myself from snorting. I'll bet they didn't.

....

Papuan tribal society is loosely structured, in the sense that heads of families and clans control their own lives within certain traditional norms. Spiritual beliefs are similarly decentralised. Bili and I have found a way round the elder women's reluctance to say where the girl has come from. We hit upon it by chance. When we'd been admiring the mummified bodies of Suamu forebears, our attention had been drawn by the women to one particular man who'd died three years ago. His name was Bodenda. It was obvious that he was revered above all others. Scheldt would almost certainly have met him, and when I checked, sure enough, she had noted down some of her conversations with him. This is what she wrote.

"Bodenda is more than a leader of the men. The women respect him too. Normally they guard their own power jealously, but it seems that Bodenda is close to being a chief of the whole tribe. He is also a shaman." It's interesting that Scheldt quotes Bodenda as referring to Gogola as "she" and "her". This girl seems to meet some, but not all, of the requirements: terrible to look at, female, and coming from far away, as the women we spoke to had confirmed. What is unproven so far is that she has come from over the sea.

Scheldt had also recorded that Bodenda had told her that Golgola would speak powerfully and forcefully when she arrived, but that the Suamu wouldn't be able to understand what she said. That contradicted the rest of the evidence. She's as mute as a swan.

But whatever the evidence or lack of it, two things are indisputable. Golgola was foretold by Bodenda, and Golgola is what they call this girl.

....

Hellified shit! The Walukek have only gone and attacked the Suamu. Not here in the village, not to rescue me, but down in some valley. It wasn't like the last time, with warriors putting on their bling and doing a war dance before they whooped and hopped off into the forest. No, this time they rushed out like a swarm of angry wasps, having grabbed their spears, bows, and arrows. I'm so used to thinking I'm allowed to go anywhere that I thought I might be able to join them, Athena leading her troops into battle. But two of the women elders came up and restrained me. So what I did was stand where the warriors could see me. They streamed past, and as they did so, each man raised his bow or spear in a sort of salute, which I returned with my papal blessing. I was aware that Toffee-nose and her skivvy were watching me, so I was careful not to say anything in English. Instead, I went something like 'Hi-hoo-wah' in my most imperious tone until they'd all gone. Now I'm waiting for the result. I'm thinking of Ekapamne and her husband. I do hope he goes home safe.

It was no good asking Bili; she wouldn't understand, but I distinctly saw it. The girl was definitely blessing them with the sign of the cross. And the men, for all their rushing, were saluting her with their bows and spears as they ran past her. When I asked what she was shouting out, Bili said it wasn't in any language that she knew.

Of course it was no good asking if I could witness the battle. Even the Suamu elder women aren't allowed to see it. Jameson witnessed several, but he was a man. Wherever one goes in the world, even to the farthest corners, women's rights are still suppressed.

But that sign of the cross? The movements are very specific. It cannot be a coincidence that she was making them, can it?

....

I could just hear the sounds of the battle in the distance through the trees. My agony was that I didn't want any of my fam to be killed, whether Walukek or Suamu. After what happened before, I knew what to expect, which only made it worse.

The tone changed in late afternoon from chaotic screams and whistles to rhythmic chanting which grew gradually louder. They were coming home. I tried to gauge the mood and decided that it sounded triumphant. But would that mean that the Walukek had had the shit kicked out of them? Sickened, I took up a position by where the track entered the village. The women, children, and old men gathered behind me, making sure that I was standing at the

138

front. The stuck-up cow and her calf stood opposite watching me. They just had to go poking their noses into everything I was doing.

The warriors emerged from the forest grinning and shaking their weapons. This time, instead of merely raising their spears and bows at me as they rushed past, each stood in front of me in turn with arms wide and did a sort of dipping bow. A few smiled and one or two grinned. I decided it wasn't appropriate for Athena or Golgola to smile back, so I tilted my head and looked down my nose, giving each warrior a nod which I hoped was a sign of both approval and dismissal. The last warrior of all, a magnificent figure of a man, actually laughed in triumph. It was that which made me realise for sure that the Suamu had been victorious. OMG, where were the wounded and the bodies? There weren't any. It seemed that every warrior had returned unscathed. Perhaps they think it's down to me.

....

I now have conclusive proof. This woman with a mangled face is Golgola, as predicted by the late leader Bodenda. All the women we've spoken to agree that she came from far away. They also insist that she came from over the sea, however improbable that may seem. She speaks a language no one here understands, Bili has been assured of that. That's surprising, as we haven't heard her utter more than three words. If she came from over the sea, she is hardly likely to speak Suamu, especially as she has only been here for two months.

That evidence of her speaking doesn't stack up. I've checked, and Scheldt definitely recorded that Golgola would speak powerfully and forcefully, even though she wouldn't be understood. I don't trust Scheldt. She's either misinterpreted what she was told or made that part up. This creature has uttered nothing more than "Hi-hoo-wah".

....

One of the senior women tried to tell me something which I couldn't understand. So when I spoke a few words of Walukek, she brought in another woman and between us I found out that there's to be a great ceremony in two days' time. They kept pointing to me and doing that palm forward salutation, so I guessed they were telling me that I would be the guest of honour. Suits me. It seems I've brought them a great victory. I've been told that two Walukek were killed in an ambush and several wounded. That doesn't make me feel good, but there's nothing I can do about it.

If I knew how, I'd use my authority to make a special request that Madam Toffee-nose be kept well away.

....

Bili's been told that the Suamu were victorious over the Walukek, who suffered heavy casualties. There's to be a big feast to celebrate the victory in two days' time. Meanwhile I need to get on with my other fieldwork. I mustn't get side-tracked by this one subject, who's atypical, which is the anthropological word for a freak. And she isn't even a Suamu.

....

The crowd is huge, even bigger than during my ceremony three days after I'd arrived. I think the whole tribe must be here. I've got on all my bling, exotic feathers swaying as I move. I must look fantastic. I've been led up to my throne in front of the altar. They're all looking at me. I am Athena. I am Golgola. I am a Goddess, Queen of the Spirits. I am terrible. I will take control.

....

What my fellow anthropologists and rivals would have given to witness that. It was completely Papuan and yet not. The girl was led up to a sort of throne made of rushes and bark behind the big stone. She looked resplendent, in spite of her injuries. Everyone, warriors, elders, women, and children, had been decorated in their most expressive tribal costumes. A sinister hissing noise had been growing in intensity. Suddenly it stopped.

The girl stood up and threw her arms out wide.

'Professor Coulter! Professor Coulter! You're a complete arsehole and a twitty-twat.'

Low murmuring from the people sounded approving.

'I am the great Athena. Huh? Professor Kovacs, Professor Dollen, you worship at my shrine.'

I glanced at Bili. She must obviously be

recognising some of the English words, but to her the sentences must have seemed gobbledegook.

'Sod the past, embrace the present.' She threw back her head. 'Now.'

I was thrashing around in my brain trying to understand what she was up to. I thought I'd got it. She's English, she's been thrown into a situation where she's been forced to act, I mean act in the theatrical sense. Her words don't matter, she just has to say something, anything, that sounds commanding.

She came down from her throne and was strutting around clapping in front of the arc of people facing her. As she passed each group in turn, they saluted her in that way which I've seen them use to greet her, palms forward. The effect was like a Mexican wave.

She returned to the stone and without warning put her hands together in front of her face, bowed her head, and then crumpled into a curtsey. It was graceful and, I have to say, beautiful. After half a minute she unfolded, stepped back onto her throne, and sat motionless, her head bowed into her lap.

There was complete silence. Then one of the female elders walked to the front and gave a signal with her hand. Four pigs were led squealing to the stone. The girl stood up briefly and blessed them with the sign of the cross. An archer shot each pig in turn with varying degrees of effectiveness, one of them escaping its handler and bolting into the crowd with an arrow sticking out, before dropping down dead.

A large portion of the crowd melted away, while

the others relaxed and stood at ease. There was much activity and inactivity until I realised that they were preparing for the feast.

. . . .

I think I did that well. I didn't want to go on too long, just enough to show some power before passing the initiative back to them. What Snooty-nose made of it I haven't a clue. It's her problem, not mine.

. . . .

It's late in the evening. Bili has retired to our *ebeai*. Flying sparks have given way to collapsing embers. The dancing finished twenty minutes ago. I tried to get to the girl, but she slunk away without saying goodbye to anyone, back to her hut at the edge of the forest. I must try to speak to her in the morning. I need to find out why she thinks she needs to do this and how much she's their prisoner. I believe she could be in danger. The pendulum will swing the other way sooner or later.

The cat's out of the bag, to use a bum-arsed cliché. I mean, Lady Tits-in-the-air now knows I speak English. There's no point in avoiding her anymore.

....

I met her coming towards me. Bili wasn't with me, and I was glad. This needed to be a conversation between two Englishwomen. She stopped but didn't try to turn away. She stood before me motionless. Gone was her elaborate decoration of the previous night, replaced by the frightfulness of her injuries, now made worse by her frozen stare.

'Who are you?'

Only her ghastly lips moved. Her speech was fluffy and indistinct. 'I am Golgola.'

'That's what they call you. But it's not who you are, is it?'

She didn't answer that. 'I know all about you. It seems that my research is better than yours. You're Dr Rachel Atkinson *MBE*.' She spat the last letters at me. Her sarcasm hurt. 'But you do know about me. I'm mentally disabled, repulsive to look at, and dumb. I have it on good authority: you.'

I wasn't used to being spoken to like that. She might well require my help, so she needed to be civil. I was in a position of professional responsibility, so if I decided that she warranted my support, I would have to give it to her. But I would need some respect from her first.

I was aware of her escorting lady staring at us from just a few metres away. She must be realising that we were understanding each other. But at least she couldn't know what we were saying. 'What is your real name?'

'People call me Athena, but my real name is Awhina Fernandez.'

'How come you're here? Look, can we go somewhere private?'

'You can come to my house. That woman will follow us, but I doubt if she'll enter.'

Her hut was small, dark and stuffy. Was it my imagination, or was there a faintly feline smell? I listened to her story. In spite of her muffled voice, I could understand all of what she was saying. Years of listening to unfamiliar accents and dialects have made me skilled in adapting to different sound formations. Her voice was much more indistinct than it was out there when making her speech. I've studied and lectured in phonology. When projecting one's voice, it's impossible to amplify consonants much, so it's the vowels which can be made much louder. Since vowel sounds aren't so dependent on movement of the lips, she had no problem in declaiming reasonably well to a large audience in the open air. Many women can't project their voices powerfully enough, but she did it well.

'Where did you come from and how did you get here?'

'I was on a cruise with my mother. I think I must have gone swimming underwater and hit something which tore into my face. Umpanu, he's a chief of the Walukek, told me that some boatmen rescued me and brought me to his village.'

I couldn't help looking astonished. 'You've been with the Walukek?'

For the first time I saw a smile flutter around the distorted face. 'I spent two months with them. They saved my life and I love them.'

'So how did you get here?'

'I was working with some women in the fields. Four Suamu warriors with spears surrounded us. It was soon clear that it was me they were after. I was captured and brought here.'

'Do you know why?'

'Haven't a clue. I thought they were going to torture, rape, kill, or eat me. Then they had a huge ceremony. I decided to play badass, so I shouted and waved my fists at them. They seemed to like that, because from then on they've treated me very well and seem to have a sort of reverence of me.'

'I know why.'

Her chaotic mouth dropped open in different directions and her eyes widened. 'You do?'

I told her all about the prophesy of Bodenda as recounted by Scheldt, how he'd foretold that this female spirit called Golgola would come to the Suamu from over the sea. Golgola would be fearful to look at. She would speak powerfully but they would not understand the words. Golgola's arrival would be a great day for the tribe and would bring them good fortune.

'But I didn't arrive, as you put it. I was captured and brought here.'

'That's right. Somehow the Suamu must have found out that you were with the Walukek and fitted the description. They coveted you.'

'I don't think I like the idea of being coveted.'

'What did you say your name was?'

'Awhina Fernandez. My friends call me Athena.'

'So, Athena, what are your expectations and what do you hope to do next?'

'I'm well-treated here, but I don't want to stay. I'm a science graduate at Cambridge University, waiting to start my PhD. I desperately want to get back to my research and networking.'

'Which you can't do here with no internet. You've told me what you want. Now, what do you think will happen to you?'

'I don't know.'

'Athena, I don't want to frighten you, but I think you could be in danger. Why do you think we had that ceremony today when they gathered in huge numbers to honour you?'

'Because they'd won a victory over the Walukek and thought that I was responsible for it?'

'Precisely. So who would have got the blame if they'd lost?'

She was giving me that frozen stare which I'd seen before. It took a lot of effort to return her gaze sympathetically when it looked as though she was assessing me with evil contempt, but I had to. Her muffled speech didn't help. 'You're saying that the Suamu will only tolerate me as long as things are going well for them?'

'I'm suggesting that, yes.'

This time her eyes widened. 'Did Scheldt record Bodenda as saying how it would end for Golgola?'

For the first time, I realised what sort of person I was talking to. I'd only mentioned Scheldt and Bodenda once, yet she'd recalled their names and who they were. And it was an extremely intelligent question.

'Not exactly. But Scheldt did write that Golgola's presence within the tribe would be short.'

'Sweet Jesus, fucking shit. I'm stuffed then.'

'I can help you.' I didn't know how, but I realised I'd misjudged this damaged creature. She could be useful to me in the future. I'd gone there as an anthropologist, but I was also a film producer. Her experiences were so extraordinary that I might be able to make a documentary about her adventures.

She changed the subject. 'Who's that woman you're with?' Was it my imagination, or had her tone softened?

'Bili? She's my translator. She's a Suamu, but she speaks Walukek too.'

'How long are you here for and what are you doing?'

'I'm researching the Suamu and Walukek in turn, spending a month with each. I'm particularly interested in their relationship.'

She let out a puff of air. 'I can answer that: shitty.'

I tried to humour her. 'There are anthropological nuances to the word "shitty".'

After the contempt she'd shown me before, I expected her to sneer, and was surprised when she nodded with a lopsided smile.

One of the female elders entered unannounced, followed by a sheepish-looking Bili. The woman saluted Athena, then turned to me. Bili translated. 'She says you must leave.'

That was ambiguous. 'Leave where? Leave this house or leave this village?'

I couldn't tell whether the woman's frown was due to confusion or agitation. 'Leave now.'

No clarification there. I decided to make my own interpretation. 'Come, Bili.' To Athena I said, 'Don't worry, I won't abandon you.' I stood up tall, gave what I hoped was an assertive glance at the woman, and strode out towards the *silis*. The request to leave Golgola's hut might have been reasonable, but I wasn't going to leave the village without an official request from the assembled elders. I ostentatiously squatted in the centre of my *sili* where all could see me and started writing up my notes.

. . . .

After Rachel had breezed out followed by her Bili, I decided to exert some authority of my own. I faced the woman, put my hands on my hips, and uttered a loud, 'Huh!' Then I flapped my hands at her and wafted her out of the room. That by itself wasn't enough. I needed to make it clear that Golgola wasn't going to be pushed around. The whole tribe must know that Golgola speaks to whoever she chooses. I ducked out of my hut and marched to the centre of the village. My lady-in-waiting couldn't keep up. Rachel wasn't there, so I strutted off to her enclosure, where I planned to extract her from her sleeping quarters and let them all see that I, Golgola, had chosen to be with this woman. Instead, I found Rachel sitting outside writing, so I stood over her.

I'd caught a glimpse of Athena's intellect back at her hut. Now I was to experience just how brilliantly her mind worked. She saw what needed to be done far more clearly than I did.

'Get up!' she shouted at me.

I clambered to my feet.

'Salute me now, palms forward, the way the others do. Come with me. Don't speak, don't look at me. If we stop, turn to me and salute me. Bili, you stay here.'

I nodded my agreement to Bili, who looked puzzled and hurt.

We walked through the village, and every time we passed another *sili*, we paused, I saluted, and Athena shouted expletives at me in English at the top of her voice. Men, women, and children came out to see what was going on, including some of the elders. I knew what she was doing. She was confirming her status and letting the whole village know that I too was her subject, not her confidante. That way our presence together would be accepted. Clever.

When we were some way beyond the central clearing and almost alone, she said quietly without looking at me, 'Meet me an hour after sunrise where the mummies are. Look as though you're discussing them with me. Don't bring Bili.' She smirked crookedly through her distorted lips. 'No one messes with Golgola. I'm leaving you now. Tomorrow we'll walk together in the forest and make our plans. Salute me once more.'

'You did that well,' I breathed.

'Yes.' She glided off towards her hut.

Athena and I were standing close together pretending to discuss the mummies. One of her female attendants was squatting a few metres away and, beyond her, stood a warrior with bow and arrows.

'If you're going to move on to the Walukek in three weeks' time, can I go with you?'

'The question is, will they let you?'

'I could escape and join you near the border.'

'We need to think carefully about that. If they caught you, anything could happen.'

'I'm up for it.'

I only just prevented myself from turning sharply towards her. The recklessness of youth, I thought. 'You know I told you last night that you could be in danger if the Suamu had some bad luck and blamed you for it?'

She remained silent, staring at the mummies.

'In the short-term it's better for you than I'd indicated. You have the victory over the Walukek in the battle, but there's been another piece of good fortune in the past week. I told her all about my meeting in Jakarta and the fact that I'd managed to stop the gold mining.

'I'm a trustee of a charity which deals with such things, and I also have contacts high up in…'

'Of course you do. Contacts are what got you your MBE. It's not what you know but who you know, and how far you're prepared to prostitute yourself to get it.'

It was as though she'd slapped me in the face. I wasn't used to being insulted like that. Tact obviously wasn't Athena's strong suit. I decided that showing offence would make no impression on her.

'Nevertheless,' I said sternly, 'they might attribute that success too to Golgola's arrival.'

'Have they said that?'

'No. they haven't,' I admitted, 'but they may be thinking it.'

'Then we can't take it into account.'

She was right. I had only mentioned it to comfort her. Or had I? I was proud at what I'd achieved and wanted some recognition. Clearly, I wasn't going to get it from Ms Athena Fernandez. I now realised how that disciplined brain of hers worked. Her scientific mind needed facts, not comfort, and pride in the Establishment was a turn-off.

We needed to plan her escape. I was still thinking about that documentary I could make. She would be strong material, if she survived. That wasn't my only motive for helping her. For all the disdain she'd shown towards me, I respected her courage and intellect. My desire to protect her out of duty had mutated into something more than that. Although I couldn't express it, I now felt a strong emotional attraction towards her. I cared deeply about what might happen to her, and thoughts of the perils she was facing had become an obsession.

....

Here's the plan. Rachel will be leaving with Bili in a week's time. We've decided there's no way the Suamu will let me go with them. If I asked, they would only step up their security. We've also concluded that if I were to break out within hours of their departure, it would look like a put-up job. So I'm going to escape by myself tonight, a week earlier. That means Rachel can express surprise and disappointment at my treachery. And if I do get captured, she might be able to help me, though how, neither of us really knows. Bili hasn't been told, partly for her own protection and partly because the Suamu might be impressed by her genuine surprise when she finds out that I've disappeared. Also, and this may be being unfair to her, Bili's a Suamu and we have to take into account that her loyalties might be towards them, tempting her to tip them off. So, I'm going to do a runner tonight and hopefully reach Walukek territory early tomorrow. I know where it is, although moving around in the forest at night with all those creepie-crawlies and a pack of warriors on my tail will be butt-clenchingly scary. But I'm up for it. I'm worried about my feet, though. I'm used to walking around barefoot, and my soles have hardened in recent months. But the idea of running through the forest in the dark, tarantulas squelching between my toes, and poisonous snakes slithering up my legs, does give me the squitter-jabs.

All I'll have with me will be a small dark bilum bag containing a torch which Rachel has lent me and some pepper spray which apparently she carries around with her on her travels. Those are all my worldly possessions, except that they're not mine. Rachel's warned me that the torch will soon become dim and run out of juice. That could be my fate too.

PART VII

It started quite well. We'd chosen a night when the moon would be at its fullest. Although it was cloudy, diffused light penetrated the mist, so I could see the outline of trees. The temperature was perfect, warm and still. I got up sometime around midnight, walked to the entrance of my hut, and gave a commanding 'Huh' to the warrior who was guarding me. I blew a farty raspberry and pointed to my butt. There couldn't be much doubt about what that meant. With the guard following, I walked through the silent forest about a hundred metres further than normal. He didn't object. I squatted without undoing anything, hoping he was one of the polite ones who looked away. He was. The trees towered above me. For all my excitement, I could appreciate the night scents drifting in the soft air, and the silence. I would need my senses in full functioning order.

It was now or never. I stood up and ran down an open area of grassland. The warrior let out a cry of surprise and then he started chasing me, as I'd known he would.

I'd gambled there was no way he was going to thrust his spear into Golgola. Rather, he would point it at me and assume I'd be intimidated enough to go with him back to the village. I grabbed the shaft as though trying to wrestle it off him, even though I had no chance of doing so. He reacted exactly as I'd hoped he would. After a short tussle, he wrenched the spear from my hands, flung it away, and stood staring at me with a wolfish grin. Then he started to close in. I waited until he was just about to seize me, then gave him a prolonged squirt in both eyes with Rachel's pepper spray. He gave a yell and jumped back, clutching his face. I'd promised myself that I wasn't going to use his spear on him. He'd been temporally blinded, but just to give myself even more time, I gave him a well-aimed kick in the nuts. Big mistake. Instead of running back to get help, he screamed loud enough to wake the whole village. I'd lost a precious couple of minutes.

I turned and ran off down the remainder of the grassland, using Rachel's torch. Several recces over the past week had shown me there was a stream ahead. My plan had been to wade fifty metres to the right, in the direction of Walukek territory, make some footprints on the far side to confuse them, then double back in the direction they would least expect me to go. I'd assumed the guard would run back to the village and only then call for help. But his screaming when I'd kicked him in the goolies had caused a terrific din to erupt sooner. There wasn't time for my full plan. I turned round and started wading upstream, but the rocks were slippery. I stumbled several times, losing my balance. It was no longer safe to go on using the torch. The shouting had stopped, but I knew they must be getting near, the silent hunters, efficient, ruthless, with Golgola as their prey. Now I could hear monosyllabic words, commands, exchanges of information. Their night vision would be as powerful as anyone's on earth. They'd spent their whole lives without lights or candles.

No longer moving fast, no longer fuelled by adrenaline, I wanted to stop and listen, whereas terror was telling me to scream and run. I couldn't afford to do either. Whimpering silently, I blundered my way along the stream, trying not to swear as I slipped and fell in, soaking myself and bruising my shoulder. The torch would be a goner, hopefully not the pepper spray, but what good would that be against a large band of warriors?

All talking had stopped, but I could sense their presence closing in. A chittering noise had started up behind me. I couldn't tell whether it was an insect or some night bird, or whether it was the men quietly communicating with each other. Concentrate on the way ahead, you puss, you can't do anything about it.

Instead of slippery rocks, the bed of the stream had become smooth gravel, so that it was now possible to wade at a slow walking pace. I was forcing my legs through the water as fast as I could push them, risking the men hearing the sloshing of my feet. Soon they would guess that I'd taken to the stream. My oh-so clever idea was starting to unravel. I needed to act counter-intuitively. I knew what to do: turn back towards the village. I didn't know the way in the dark, so there was a chance I would become disorientated. But I had to do it. I stepped out of the stream onto the bank and walked backwards for fifty paces, hoping they'd think I'd been moving towards the stream rather than away from it. It was possible that more men would come down from the village by that route to join the others, but that was a risk I had to take.

My luck improved when I stumbled upon the bank where the mummies lounged and leered, ghostly in the diffused light. Knowing my way back from there, I ran towards the nearest house. I needed to be careful. Suamu have outstanding hearing. I worked my way along the outside of the compound. I could hear heavy breathing and the odd spluttering cough. Passing within only a few metres of the last house, I stepped out onto the main trail which led in the direction of Walukek territory.

I needed to put rapid distance between myself and my pursuers. There'd be five, maybe ten, minutes before they would know for certain that Golgola was no longer near the stream. Their immediate conclusion would be that I'd taken the path in the direction of the Walukek village. I needed to run, and run fast. But running was out of the question now. It had started to rain hard, and the thickened cloud had all but extinguished the light from the moon. I had to move slowly to keep my balance on the slippery surface of mud, and in the darkness it was hard to identify the twists in the path. What would the water be doing to my footprints? Were only the new ones, mine, visible to my pursuers? Or was the rain strong enough to wash those, fresh and soft, away too? I didn't know. Stop speculating, Athena, put all your effort into pressing on. Ignore the things you can't control.

How long would it be before they caught up with me? They could run in this, they were forest people, warriors, and they knew every bend and twist. They had stamina, they could lope for hours, whatever the state of the ground. And they had night vision. I would need to leave the track soon. When? Should I wait until I heard them coming up behind? No. They were silent hunters, focussed, co-ordinated, deadly, ants homing in on their victim. They would be upon me before I knew it. Ten, no, only five minutes, and then I must turn off, make a few hundred metres, remembering the direction back to the trail, then hide up until dawn.

It happened sooner than that. Vegetation, wet, sharp, was slapping and tearing against my face. Please no, not my lips again. I tripped, got up, rubbed some goo off my knee, and staggered obliquely into a tree. I knew that I'd lost the path and had stumbled into virgin forest. My upper lip was sore. It had either been slashed by some thorns or cut by hitting the tree. Fuck, fuck, fuck! Had all Umpanu's work been undone? I gingerly felt my face. There seemed to be something sticky around the mouth, but I couldn't tell if it was blood. I touched my lip and tentatively licked my finger.

Yuck! Some foul shit was burning my tongue. I might be bleeding, but I wouldn't try that again.

Should I go on and put more distance between myself and the track? No. In my confusion following my fall, followed by my face-scrape against the tree, I'd lost all sense of direction. If I went on, I might blunder onto the trail again. I would have to spend the night where I was. I sat down against a trunk, wet, shaking, and despairing. It seemed an age since I'd left my hut. When I'd worked it out, I realised it had been little over half an hour. I was still close to the Suamu village, close to Rachel and Bili, but a long way from Ekapamne.

The slapping of rain on leaves closed off every other sound. It was futile trying to listen out for the warriors, so I gave up trying. I fell asleep on a prickly bed of wet twigs, trashing Landale's bonkers variant of the Hardy-Littlewood zeta-function conjectures. The pillock seemed to think that, on the basis that two negatives make a positive, then two crappy conjectures equal proof. I dreamed I was surrounded by spiders. They weren't hairy but had smooth legs and round human faces. One of them was blue and had thick lips. OMG, Lily.

．．．．．．

Thinking I'm awake, but I'm not. Something nipping my toes, ouch. Pins and needles. Struggling to uncouple reality from another dream. Stiff, sore, body gummed up by dampness, limbs immobilised by cold. Realising where I am. They haven't caught me; that's good. I'm still deep in their territory;

that's bad. They won't have given up. I need to find the effort to stand up. I'll lie here a little longer. Sun is shining through dappled leaves, a bit of warmth.

A persistent chirruping nearby, "peet-peet, peet-peet-peet". Opening my eyes, blinking. Fluffy bird pecking its way through leaf litter. Round body, plump, like a small chicken with a rounded bum. Stripey, cute. I like you, little birdie. Come closer, I want to stroke your ginger coiffe. But perhaps you're not so cuddly after all. Your beak is a bit gross, and the size of your eyes, mmm, and that scaly patch on your head, make you look reptilian. Your feet are definitely oversized, as though they belong to a bird three times as big.

A vast claw slammed onto the ground a few feet from my head. WTF, a dinosaur. Splayed toes, scaly, heavy. Massive pin-sharp claws shining in the sunlight. Looking up in terror, seeing black feathers curving down towards my face. Higher still, towering over me, bare-headed, sky-blue and brick-red scaly neck, white face, and ginormous dome of a helmet. A cassowary! Rachel had pointed one out in the distance during one of our walks. Yaku had told me that they could rip one's entrails out with one swipe of that massive central claw, and that a woman had been killed by one just three years earlier. And here I am, a stride and a strike away from this monster. But Rachel had also said that their reputation for being aggressive was exaggerated. They were only really dangerous if cornered or protecting their young, and nearly all the people who'd been killed by them had fallen onto the ground. Thanks a bunch, Rachel. Here I am, having had a cooee with her chick a few feet away, and I'm lying in the dirt. Two alternatives. Not to move a muscle. I'm good at freezing. But what if they come nearer? Mum wouldn't need to claw out my entrails; she could simply put out one gigantic foot and stamp on my head. Why didn't that fucking asteroid make a proper job of wiping out the dinosaurs?

Or I could put my hand in my bilum bag and reach for Rachel's pepper spray. Don't make me do it, birdie. If I move my hand oh-so slowly… ah, so you don't like me doing that, do you? Her monstrous head with its questioning eye swings down towards me. I'm glad you've warned me, birdie. Any movement of my hand into my bag and out again, followed by finding the right trigger position on the spray, would take far too long. In this shoot-out, you could out-draw me before I'd started to move. In any case, the spray would nowhere near reach your eyes from my position on the ground. All I can do is freeze and hope.

The chick was moving away from my head but closer to my feet. Don't move a muscle, Athena, not even your eyes. You can do it, you're good at it. The chick raised its head, turned towards my foot, paused, and looked as though it was going to take a peck at my ankle. Mother was passing six feet away, parallel to her young. Without warning, the chick turned and scuttled towards its parent, as though frightened by something, perhaps my smell. My feet probably did pong a bit. Slowly, so agonisingly slowly, they wandered off.

Pepper spray in hand, I clambered slowly to my

feet, eyes never leaving the adult bird. They were still only twenty metres away, not far enough. Hearing voices behind me, not loud but close by, I swung slowly round from the hip. Warriors were moving beyond some scrubby vegetation. In my weakened state, it was difficult to keep my balance, when my feet were pointing one way and my shoulders had swivelled round the other. All depended now on my footprints from the previous night. If they could see where I'd deviated from the track, they would find me immediately. But even if they couldn't see where I'd turned off, they would notice within minutes that the prints had stopped. Either way, they would very soon start casting around. Whatever happened I'd be toast if I stayed here. I waited until the men had barely moved out of sight, then sprinted in the opposite direction, which was straight at the cassowaries. I couldn't shout a warning or the warriors would hear me. I was closing in on the birds fast, pepper spray in hand. Move birdies, move, don't make me do it. The adult looked up, seeing me bearing down on her. The problem was her chick. Mum could run off, but she would never abandon her baby. Only ten metres short, I veered off to the left between two large trees. Out of the corner of my eye, I saw the monster turn towards me. Resisting the temptation to hide behind the biggest trunk, I ran on until I was past them, and only then did I turn. The mother was coming straight at me. My split-second decision was to run some more, swivel round to face her, then use my spray. When I next turned, the mother was running back to her chick.

I knew I was only a few hundred metres from the trail and about twenty minutes' walk from the Suamu village. I needed to put distance between myself and the path. The sun, shining through the trees, would show me the direction towards Walukek territory.

I was running further away from the trail, down an increasingly steep and rocky slope. Large trees had given way to thicker, shrubby vegetation. Putting my hands up to protect my eyes from thorns, I felt thick webs clinging to my fingers. It was impossible not to think of spiders hitching a ride, exploring the best places to inject poison into my face.

The ground became so steep and rough that I couldn't run any more but had to scramble and slide into what was becoming a ravine. It obviously contained the stream I'd waded in the night before. I couldn't follow its course; it was too rocky, and anyhow I hadn't gone far enough.

It took more than three hours to climb up the bank on the other side. The combination of boulders and thorny vegetation prevented me from making more than a few metres at a time, and I was constantly having to pull back and find a different route. Several times I got caught up in creepers from which I could only extricate myself by tearing my skin. Large yellow and brown striped insects were buzzing round me, and every bush seemed coated in thick cobwebs which clung to my face, legs, and chest. My foot had slipped off a boulder early on, so that my knee was bleeding heavily. I watched a snake slide into a hole as though someone inside had sucked on spaghetti. Big yikes. Ekapamne had said that the most poisonous of all was that colour, light brown.

As I finally hauled myself over the lip of the ravine, I pinned my hopes on a bare hill I'd spotted from the other side, a mile or two ahead. I hoped it was sufficiently in the wrong direction to confuse my pursuers, but not so far as to take me back towards the Suamu village.

Leaving the scrub, I paused at the edge of open grassland. Climbing to the top of the hill would have the advantage that I would leave few footprints. Also, it was high enough to survey the surrounding terrain and decide the best route towards the Walukek. But it was horribly exposed. If I went straight up from where I was, my pursuers would have sight of me for at least ten minutes. But if I turned left and kept tight to the edge of the scrub, I could approach the summit in a three-minute sprint.

It was highly risky, but I went for it. I'd intended to spend no more than a minute or two on top, choose my route, and then hurtle down the other side. I'd estimated I could reach the trees in about six minutes. My dark skin, hair, and clothes would give me some camouflage. Rapid movement would catch the eye of anyone remotely nearby, but I couldn't afford to move slowly.

Panting to the top of the hill, I swung round to the right, the direction of the Walukek. Clouds, torn and fluffy, rested lightly on the treetops. And there, far, far away, light was shining where blue met blue: the sea. I remembered what Rachel had said. "They believe that Golgola will come from over the sea, which is strange, because the Suamu aren't near the sea. It's about eight hours' walk away through Walukek territory."

I squinted through the haze. The coast looked ten, maybe fifteen, miles away. If I could get a little over half that distance, I would be clear of the Suamu and safe. After taking a mental photograph, I started to turn, ready to dash down towards the forest. Out of the corner of my eye, a splash of colour made me pause and peer. A group of women ahead and to my right swam into my consciousness. They were a long way off, but I could tell they were looking at me.

Every adult in every Suamu village would know who Golgola was. By now, word would have got around that she was on the run. Those women down by the edge of the forest wouldn't be able to see the detail of my face at that distance. But why had a lone female been sprinting up a hill? She could only be Golgola. I needed to alter course, not directly away from the Walukek, but considerably further to the left than I'd intended. Now, instead of just the warriors from my village, other Suamu would soon be chasing me. There was no point in nonchalantly walking off down the slope; I might as well run. It was getting late in the day. In an hour or so it would be dark. What I had to do was put as much distance as I could between myself, the warriors chasing me, and the women ahead to my right, without deviating too far from the direction of the sea. As if I didn't have enough to worry about, I must also avoid leaving footprints. And evade snakes, spiders, and dinosaurs.

For the second time, I saw something just as I was about to take off. Four Suamu men had joined the women and were pointing at me up the slope. I let out a little squeak of terror, then adrenaline took over. The chase was on. Only darkness could save me now, but sunset was still an hour away. It isn't easy to think hard when one's sprinting. It isn't easy to think hard when one is dehydrated and weak from hunger. Perhaps thinking wasn't what I did. Maybe it was now down to instinct. A grassy spur ran down, not away from the Suamu below, but at right angles. I careered down the ridge until I entered the forest. The Suamu would have seen that, so I calculated that the forest would be where they would start looking for me. Instead of running on through the trees, I doubled back to my left and out onto the shoulder of the hill. I was now out of sight of the warriors, running deeper into Suamu territory, away from the Walukek. But I was on grass, where footprints would hopefully be invisible. Also, I was now on the eastern side of the hill, where darkness would fall soonest. And I'd guessed that the hill itself would be the last place where the warriors would expect me to be. Now I needed to find a place to spend another miserable night.

. . . .

I had an overwhelming thirst, my lips were even more cracked than usual, and my tongue was sticking to the inside of my mouth. I should have stopped to drink at that stream. The previous night, with all the rain, I'd been able to take in a fair amount of water. But throughout the day, the sun had shone relentlessly, and I'd become dangerously dehydrated. Hunger was clenching me, and a hollow feeling in my gut was making me queasy. Every few minutes, an intense cramping pain twisted through my stomach. I couldn't imagine how I was going to be able to sleep, even though I should have been tired enough to zonk out immediately. Kipping out in open grassland in the moonlight would have been suicidal. I'd cast around at the edge of the forest and found a place where I was protected on three sides. I could only be spotted by someone close by, but I'd left footprints. I tried to scuff them out but in doing so I laid more. Too weak and exhausted to continue, I'd given up trying.

My shelter was more of a concave scrape in a cliff than a cave, but the ground wasn't too wet and there was a good supply of leaves. Better still, I'd found clumps of tall grass, easy to pull up, as a sort of bedding. It was all very scratchy, though, and my skin was chafing from stale sweat, boils, thorns, and insect bites. Stomach cramps, thirst, sores, and itchiness were all fighting so hard with each other that my brain had given up trying to identify them all. I was beginning to feel numb and anaesthetised, and a sort of hot ache was passing through me in waves.

I'm not really asleep, or am I? I can hear that spooky whistling sound, the one the massed Suamu made on the night of my terrifying ceremony, when I'd thought I was going to be killed in a ritual. It's coming from close by. I'm lying here terrified but unable to move. Best not to move. They may be near, but they might not find me if I lie still. Freeze, don't move, it's your answer to everything. They're leading Ekapamne to that stone altar. They're laying her down, face up on the slab. She's smiling. A more fearsome warrior than I've ever seen before is holding a stone axe and leering down at her. Only I, Golgola, can save her. But I can't, I've frozen.

I sat up with a jerk, breathing heavily, leaves and grass exploding all around. It was cupboard-with-the-door-shut dark. My head was throbbing, and it felt as though my blood was just below boiling point. My bedding had been scattered in all directions, and finding it was impossible in the dark.

I spent the next hour listening for sounds beyond my shallow breathing, until exhaustion must have overwhelmed me.

....

It's fully daylight, hot, and chokingly humid. Leaves and twigs are sticking to sweat, and I don't like the pong coming from my armpits and groin. The cicadas are deafening, and I can also hear that bell-like bird with the tumbling notes, the one I'd listened to from my hut at the edge of the Suamu village. It's so beautiful lying on my back, staring up at the dappled sunlight. There's no need to go

169

anywhere. Just stay comfortable, Athena. Take your time. Plan how you're going to spend your day. A mojito would be nice. With David. Perhaps not.

It's taken me a long time to face up to reality. My options are stark. To the west, the direction I need to go, the hill rises up, bare and exposed. I cannot go there. The forest to the south is where they would most likely expect me to be, because that's where they last saw me, so that's out too. Walking to the east would be safe at first, but it would take me deeper into Suamu territory, not far from the main village, and away from the Walukek. My only hope lies to the north. Even that is a horrible option. I will have to tackle the ravine again, climb up the slope, and cross the track which I left thirty-six hours ago. I will actually be closer to the Suamu village than I'd been then. Tears are filling my eyes thinking about it. All the terror and hardship of the past day and two nights will have got me nowhere.

The sun has been up for several hours. At last I've stood up, tottered, and sat down again. It's so beautiful here, with the buzzing of insects and the songs of exotic birds. A numbing drowsiness is soothing me. My various pains have become a single, anaesthetised ache.

Watching an unreal bird with white, eggy yellow, chestnut, black, and so many colours I've given up trying to remember them all, sky blue, I think, swinging and dipping on a branch. Feeling a tickling across my thigh. Looking down and seeing a giant, I mean, really ginormous, centipede. Screaming and jumping up, my yells echoing off the cliff behind me. Realising that maybe someone must have heard my shrieks, amplified by the vertical rock. Perhaps they have.

I'm trying to concentrate on what I must do: enter the ravine, drink from the stream, drink more, drink until drinking becomes unpleasant, climb the slope, find the track which leads between the main Suamu and Walukek settlements, cross it very carefully, go a few hundred metres into the forest beyond, turn left, and walk towards Walukek territory, keeping the sun on my left, if it's still shining.

Running along a path through orange and blue butterflies after hearing voices all around me. What happened after that? I don't know. All emotion had disappeared: fear, anticipation, frustration. I no longer cared what happened to me. Just enjoy the mojitos. I couldn't recall the big picture, only minutiae. There was a stream with a waterfall, dragonflies, streamlined birds swooping and swerving. Did I swim there or drink? I must have drunk, for how else could I have survived?

Stepping on something, what? A pain rocketing up from my big toe, so intense that it seemed to penetrate my whole body. Crumpling down onto the ground, writhing in pain. Lying there twitching for how long? Feeling my left leg go numb. Later, running my fingers around my ankle, feeling it rounded, swollen, hot. My foot no longer painful, just numb. Swollen more than ever, nasty green and brown. That must have been later. Finding a dead branch, perfect height for a crutch. Hobbling along a path, not thinking it safer to be off it. Realising much later, I'd left my bilum bag with Rachel's things somewhere. Which way was I going? The sun on my left, the sun on my left. Stumbling upon some cultivated beds, recognising taro, sweet potato, and bananas. Thinking, what did Yaku and Ekapamne say about eating raw taro? Choosing sweet potato instead, to be safe. Rough, dry, hard, difficult to chew and swallow with no saliva. Bananas only a little softer, almost as starchy. Thinking they're not bananas. Plantain?

Three dogs, brown, with faces like hyenas, rushing at me, tails wagging, snarling, teeth bared, surely couldn't be both? Knocked over. Putting my hands up to my face, waiting to be mauled by bites which never came. A man shouting. Thinking, it's over. Not to worry. I'm still Golgola. At least I tried my best. Rachel will still be there, and Bili, they'll protect me.

....

A face was staring down at me, swimming in and out of focus. A man, not young. OMG, it was Umpanu, serious as ever. Then it was Yaku, smiling, but her smile looked anxious, forced. What had I done? Then it was Ekapamne. I tried to rise, but a restraining hand was placed on my shoulder. I wanted to hug her for a week.

I'd been sedated. More days passed, how many? And then the face and the voice were Rachel's.

There were so many questions I wanted to ask. 'How did I get here?'

'You tell me. They say a man from another Walukek village found you wandering and delirious, dressed in Suamu clothes.' Why was Rachel looking so serious? 'Apparently you couldn't speak for a long time, and when you did, he was flabbergasted that you addressed him in Walukek. He brought you to this village, where you lived before. You've been here for four days. Umpanu has been treating you.'

'Umpanu's always treating me. It's all he does.' My feeble attempt at a joke made no impression on Rachel.

'Athena, this will come as a shock to you. Umpanu can only do so much. His herbal remedies have kept the infection at bay to some extent. But you need antibiotics and most likely surgery. I'm sorry. That leg of yours, we need to get you to a hospital. We've sent a runner down to the village on the coast.'

'There's no hospital there. I spent time in that village too.'

'I know. There's a man with a powerful boat who calls in there regularly. He's due in today. They're asking him to wait, so we're hoping he can take you to Sundabang. A helicopter will fly you to a hospital in Sulawesi.'

'How long have I got?'

Rachel looked shocked. 'Don't worry about that now.'

I realised she'd misunderstood my question. She must have thought I'd been asking how long I had left... to live? 'I mean how long before I leave here?' I wanted to say goodbye to Ekapamne properly.

'Oh, half an hour, maybe a bit more.'

'I want to thank you for all you've done for me.

Without you…' I started sobbing. 'I mean, I hope we'll see each other again.'

Rachel looked upset, then determined. 'You will, today, tomorrow, and the next day. I'm coming with you.'

Soon after, Ekapamne's face appeared again. I pulled her down onto me, hugging her tight. I couldn't let go of her. I was laughing and crying. She looked embarrassed and then I saw it, a tear tottering on her cheek.

Rachel gave us a few minutes more. 'Come, we've got to go now. You'll see her again.'

At the time, those words seemed meaningless. Ekapamne, my beautiful Ekapamne, was leaving my life for ever.

It was touch and go whether my left leg would have to be amputated. It wasn't, but simultaneous bouts of malaria and hepatitis should have killed me.

PART VIII

EIGHTEEN MONTHS LATER

Rachel wants to meet me. That doesn't mean I want to meet her. She's invited me to her club for lunch. Yes, her private London club, exclusive don't you know, members only. Qualifications for membership, zero merit. You have to have money, and you have to be sponsored by other members, people like yourself, to ensure the purity of the tribe doesn't get diluted. A nest of mutual arse-lickers all propping each other up.

I'd expected a revolving door, high ceilings with dingy wooden panelling, and ornate stucco. I was surprised to find it airy, with soft grey furnishing, pastel shades on the walls, glass, and modern art. Mmm, tasteful, interesting.

It had been four months since I'd last seen Athena. That was just after she'd had the third operation on her face. Having identified a top plastic surgeon to rebuild her mouth, I'd raised the money by a mixture of crowd funding and bullying her father, topped up by a financial contribution from me. Athena had been dead against it at first, because she wanted to work on her research proposal for her PhD. She also wanted to return to her networking and cultivation of contacts high up in the scientific world. I'd soon got to realise from others that she was in the top echelon of scientific thinking, admired by many in high places.

I can't be certain why she changed her mind and agreed to have the operations, but I'm guessing she was alarmed by the way people were reacting to her horrifying looks. Khalid Mudafa, the surgeon, was patient and persuasive in explaining how he could improve Athena's speech and make her look pleasant, even though her scars would always be obvious at first glance.

I'd met her parents. Her father had seemed distant, and I'd had to battle to get his attention. Her mother talked to me in front of Athena as though she wasn't there and seemed disgusted by her own daughter. The ghastly woman was overwhelmed by self-pity, as though she'd been the one who'd suffered most.

I gave my name at reception, and Rachel's. I could only see women, expensively dressed, poncing around waving their fingernails at each other.

The receptionist looked me up and down with the faintest of sneers. So that was how they treated outsiders with less than perfect faces.

. . . .

I saw Athena standing by the reception desk looking out of place. I'd forewarned her about the dress code, but she'd clearly ignored me. She was wearing a skimpy top of iridescent purple, mauve lipstick and mascara, and a short skirt of mustard yellow. If I were being kind, I would say that she looked arty.

She watched me warily. I didn't think she would look pleased to see me and she didn't. But at least her face was pleasing to look at. I'd expected much from Mr Mudafa but had never thought that he could transform her mouth to that extent. Gone were the sad expression, the sulky pout, the malevolent stare, the inability to express emotions. One would always see a disfigured face the moment one saw her, but now her demeanour was pleasant. Her positive outlook had probably saved her life. To have survived suffering from a seriously infected leg, malaria, and hepatitis all at the same time had been a miracle of resilience.

We sat down and I ordered her a mojito. 'You look great. How are you feeling?'

She ignored my question. 'What is this place?'

I explained that it was a women-only club where people could relax with old friends and meet new ones. I told her about the accommodation, the bars, restaurants, pool, gym, sauna, and jacuzzi.

'Can anyone join? Could I?'

'Do you want to?'

'No. I wouldn't want to be corrupted by mediocrity. Remember? It's not what you know but who you know. Where's the mutual back-scratching room?'

Even by her standards, that was offensive. I let it pass. 'How's your research proposal coming along?'

'Slaying it. But I'm bugging that I've missed this round and will now have to wait another year before I can get accepted.'

'Confident?'

'That I'll be accepted? Completely.'

A waitress came to take our order. Athena didn't want anything more than a chicken panini and a glass of water. I told the waitress to cancel the table in the restaurant so we could snack in the bar. 'And your networking? You told me before that you were having a meeting with Professor Dollen about a project of his.'

She leant forward and brightened. 'His theory of consequential lensing; I've developed it on from where he started. He'd said that I'd made a mistake in one of my formulae, but I hadn't. All I'd done was make an assumption without declaring it as such.'

'Sounds like you've impressed him.'

'He's offered me a job, but I've turned it down.'

I looked questioningly at her.

'As his research assistant. No thanks. I don't want to go forward on his rails. I've got my own theories which I'm developing. I can't start my PhD course for nearly another year, which is shit-arse.'

There was a long silence while she sipped her mojito. I thought this might be the moment.

....

Six months earlier, soon after Athena's second operation, the gruelling one with all the skin grafts, I'd visited her in hospital. She'd told me she hadn't been able to concentrate on her work and was, expletive deleted, bored. So she'd decided to use the time to write an account of her experiences in the Far East. She'd finished it, she said. I asked if I could see it. She gave me a pitying look but transferred the file.

I was astonished. She wrote extremely well, with good use of descriptive colour and dialogue. It almost read like a novel.

'Is this all true?' I asked when I next saw her.

'All of it.'

The reason why I believed her was that the part when we'd been together with the Suamu was exactly as I remembered it. I recalled how insulting she'd been to me at first, and here in print her impressions of me were hostile, even vicious. She'd been obsessed with my MBE, which she described as "corrupt". Reading how much she despised me was sobering, yet in a perverse way it made me admire her for her honesty.

The account started when she'd flown to Bali with her mother and ended when she'd been told that her leg might have to be amputated. She clearly despised her mother, yet strangely had agreed to go on a five-week holiday with her. I speculated that Athena's eccentric personality had been formed by a neglecting father and a domineering mother. Then I recalled that spectrum disorders such as autism don't have behavioural causes.

There were just two sections of her story which seemed deficient, and both were around the time of her accident. It troubled her that she couldn't recall how it had happened. Umpanu had told her that she'd been pulled from the sea by two fishermen. But how she'd come to be there, so horribly disfigured, she had no clue. She'd met a couple of Australians on board a few days earlier. She'd quite fancied one of them, David. She was confused as to whether she'd had sex with him, but she did say that she was both attracted and repelled by physical contact. She disliked the other Australian, Bruce. She thought he might have been molesting her when she'd had her accident, but again she was vague.

'Athena, you should get this published. It's well-written and your story is sensational.'

She didn't speak, just gave me her neutral stare. I didn't pursue it with her at the time, but already an idea was forming in my mind.

....

Now, sitting with her in my club six months later, I took a deep breath and put forward my plan.

'Athena, since you can't start your PhD course for another year, I've got a proposition for you. It should make you rich and a bit famous, and it'll be a lot of fun.'

'I don't want to be rich or famous so that I can get into this club. It doesn't interest me.'

'Like to hear what I'm offering first?'

She shrugged. That was the nearest I was going to get to approval. 'Have you thought about how staggeringly unusual your experience in Indonesia was and how fascinating it will be to most people?'

'So, you've read my account of what happened. Do you want my approval to publish it?'

'More. Much, much more than that.'

She looked vaguely curious.

'I've obtained funding to make a documentary about the Walukek and the Suamu.'

'Oh no!' She flung herself back in her chair. Her lightning mind had cottoned on, but not quite accurately. 'So, you want my permission so that you can tell my story as part of it?'

'Almost right, but not quite. More than that, I want you to star in it, appearing as yourself. It would no longer be called a documentary or even a docudrama; it would be a movie.' Before she could respond, I played my trump card. 'It would mean going out to Papua to film. You'd be with Ekapamne again.'

She froze into that stare which I'd known so well. It was no longer terrifying, but it could still penetrate. I returned her gaze, trying to look hopeful rather than apprehensive. 'You could still carry out your research and networking. You'd have access to the internet for much of the time, only not when we're with the Walukek.'

'And the Suamu? No, of course not, I won't be going there. Golgola in front of a camera would freak them out and they'd probably eat me. But my story without visiting the Suamu would have a humongous hole in it.'

'You're right, you won't be going there. It's too dangerous. I'm going back to them myself with Bili, before you visit the Walukek. I'll be filming wild shots, and I hope to catch one of their ceremonies. We'll use some of that material in the film.'

'But that will be weird if I'm not in any of the shots.'

'You'd be amazed what we can do with CGI, good costume design, make-up, and actors to play the part of a few Suamu. It won't be completely authentic, but that doesn't matter. It will no longer be a documentary; it will be a film based on a true story.'

Athena looked impressed, although of course she'd never say it. 'How far have you got with the rest of it?'

'I've arranged for a ship to be filmed for the wild shots of the cruise and a mock-up set of the interior. Umpanu's agreed to allow the Walukek to take part. He's lining up Bok and Duk.'

'What the shit are they?'

'They're the fishermen who first rescued you after you'd had your accident. They also took you back to Sundabang on your way to the hospital in Sulawesi. I'm pulling a film crew together, including a superb director and cinematographer I've worked with before, plus an agent who can drum up extras for the cruise. Bili will help prepare the Walukek.'

'Quite a budget.'

'Huge.'

'And if I say no?'

'That can be on two levels. If you say no to starring in it, I'll cry. But if you refuse permission for the film to be about you, I'll top myself. All I'd have left would be a half-baked documentary about the relationship between the Suamu and the Walukek.'

'That first option where I say yes to your using my story but no to me starring in it. You'd get an actress to play the part of Athena Fernandez?'

'I'd have to.'

'No, you fucking well will not. Rachel Atkinson, you're a bad bitch.' Two women at the next table looked round. 'I'll do it, all of it, the whole fucking lot. But I've got to be back by the early summer. When do we start?'

My heart was lurching. I'd been about to say take your time, have a think about it, let me know by the end of the week. I needed to slow her down, for my sake as much as hers. I tried to look severe. 'There are a few things first before we both make a total commitment.'

She gave me a pitying look.

'You'll need to take a screen test. Do you think you could recreate your speech sounds from when you were in Papua? I'll help you prepare for it. I've got a degree in phonology. I remember what you were like then. Your voice, by the way, sounds totally normal now. Mr Mudafa only said that he would improve your speech, not make it perfect. It seems he underestimated his own skill. You've got a lovely voice. If all goes well in the screen test, you could be the narrator as well as the lead character.

'Next, you'll need to get yourself an agent. I can help you with that too. Assuming you pass the screen test, we'll need to have a meeting with key people in the team: Tracey, the director, Lorna, her assistant, and Neil, the screenwriter. You'll like Neil. Your work with him will be crucial, because I want this to be your story with your personality.'

She didn't respond to any of that. 'I must be back by the end of May. I want that in my contract, no ifs, no buts. I don't know anything about shooting movies, but I can't see how you can get it all done by then.'

'We can. All the shooting involving you at each stage will be done with you first, I promise.'

She was staring at me, untrusting. I tried to look encouraging. 'One step at a time. First, I'll arrange that screen test and meanwhile I'll see about an agent.'

'That's two steps at a time.' She wasn't joking.

I ignored that. 'So, let's get that screen test set up. Do I have your permission to use excerpts from your manuscript for the screen test?'

'Are you considering any other candidates?'

'Two.'

'You won't be able to use them. You'd be in breach of copyright.'

'You wouldn't allow your story to be used, either for the screen test or the real thing? You'd get a lot of money for it.'

'No, I won't allow it.' She'd understood the situation instantly and had exploited it for her own benefit. She'd grasped that the movie would be worthless without her story and her permission to use it. Once she'd written her account, it was protected by copyright. Even before we'd signed a contract, she held power of veto over who could deliver it. Clever girl. I needed her to succeed at that screen test. There was no plan B.

． ． ． ． ． ． ．

It was a bit like my interview to get into Cambridge, except that there were no creaky floorboards, and we were all dressed in casual clothes. Rachel wasn't there. Tracey, the director, introduced herself, her assistant Lorna, and finally Sue, the casting director. I'd been sent three passages to learn in advance, easy, as I can memorise anything after one reading. The first was an argument with T-Rex before our meal at the Captain's Table, and my conversation with Captain Hasegawa before my charming mother pulled me away. Sue played the part of T-Rex, then the Captain. The second was part of my speech to the Suamu when I'd thought dreadful things were about to happen to me. My final test was to speak directly into the camera and describe the preparations for the feast with the Walukek after their fight with the Suamu.

We had to shoot the Suamu scene four times, because they complained that I was moving around too fast. When I explained that stomping in front of the Suamu had been part of my act, Tracey said that wasn't important for now. Did they want to know how it happened or didn't they? But there were several murmurs of approval, and even a couple of times when I was told that it was perfect.

I loved it. When I was doing the acting bits, I projected myself back to how I felt at the time. It was quite spooky.

....

I was so busy that it was easy for me to take my mind off Athena's screen test. But when Tracey did phone, nothing else mattered.

'What d'you think?'

'Where to begin...'

'Come on, Tracey, don't keep me in suspense. Will she do?'

'In many ways, she's a natural. She's got a strong personality and she sure can project it. So the answer's yes. When she's talking straight to camera, she's relaxed, with good diction. She's got a beautiful voice. Another thing she's got going for her is that she doesn't rush her lines, unlike most novices. She uses pauses to good effect, and she has a wide range of expressions. When Sue was doing dialogue with her, she displayed intelligent choices of off-cue expressions, remarkable for an amateur.'

'But?'

'There are several buts. She'll need a lot of coaching to make her realise that when she's acting there's a camera there and she needs to pay attention to where it is. She charged around the room and at times was unfilmable.'

'And?'

'She doesn't like being told what to do.'

I sighed. 'Don't tell me.'

'That's not all. She's an obstinate little cow who thinks she knows best. But her screen presence is powerful. If I can tame her, she could be memorable. There's one thing which I can't reconcile. It seems she's capable of turning on the charm and displaying an attractive personality. But when she wasn't being filmed, she made no attempt to ingratiate herself with any of us. She seemed disdainful, quite the diva. I don't think she's a team player. I think she may have problems with personal relationships. That's come out in her account, hasn't it? At times she seemed contemptuous of us, rude even. Does that ring true with you?'

I sucked in my breath. 'Completely.'

'Any clue why?'

'No,' I lied. I didn't want to create further doubts in Tracey's mind. It wasn't the time to tell her the extent of Athena's Asperger's.

....

Rachel phoned me. It wasn't a good time. I'd just got out of the shower and was drying myself while trying to think of a way round a flaw in Torrance's Theorem.

'Congratulations, you've got the job.'

'I know.'

'You mean they told you?'

'No, I just knew I'd slayed it.'

'Athena, sometimes you take self-confidence too far. They've told me there were several problems which we need to work on.'

'Which are yours, not mine. See you, Rachel.' I hung up.

....

I was quite angry. I needed to book some sessions with Athena, and I didn't like the way she'd put the phone down on me. I called her straight back.

'Yeah, whenever. Soon as you like.' She agreed to all the dates which I threw at her.

PART IX

THREE MONTHS LATER

We've finished filming in Bali, where we also shot the scenes for Sulawesi and Maluku. Tracey's told me the remaining action shots will be done in Sundabang and in the Walukek village. Only my narration will be filmed in the UK. They tell me Rachel and Bili are already with the Suamu. It's important that they get away from there before the Suamu discover that Golgola's with the Walukek. If they did find out I was there, they'd go ballistic and could turn on Rachel.

As the star of the show, and because it's all about my experiences, I should have the biggest say in what happened a couple of years ago, and how it's presented now. That's brought me hard up against Tracey. I don't dislike her, and in many ways I admire what she does, but it's my story, my personality, and I'm both narrator and the dominant lead, actually the only lead.

I was looking forward to doing my own stunts, the horse riding, wind surfing, diving, and swimming. I pointed out that I was good at all of them, but Tracey said she couldn't risk it if I got hurt early on. So I've got a stunt double, Becks, who thinks she's Superwoman, but is actually as thick as a gatepost. I suppose I couldn't have made the horse fall the way she did in the rice paddy, but when she choked getting out and fell in again, I cheered. She hates me, the dumb yat.

Another person I can't stand is Jessica, but that's for a different reason. Everyone else thinks she's charming, and I expect she is. She's playing the part of my mother, so I was determined to loathe Jessica so that I could get "in part", as they say. I think it's worked, because when I'm doing dialogue with the T-Rex, I get really fired up.

Lorna, the assistant director, is ok, but the person I really get on with is Neil, the screenwriter. We're a team. He totally accepts it's my story and only wants to change it if there's a really good reason. He doesn't just explain why he's writing something, he listens to me and is perfectly willing to adapt to my thinking. The most startling change we've made so far is to combine the characters of David and Bruce. And here's the thing. When we get to Sundabang, which is where we're going next, David will be there playing the part of himself merged with Bruce. I'm trying not to think of what it will be like meeting him again. I'm squirmy with anticipation.

We were about to shoot the scenes inside the ship, because that was where they'd built the set, on Sundabang.

I was lying on the beach, careless of whether my dark skin would frazzle. The wi-fi signal was good, but the sunlight was dazzling, so that it was hard to see my screen. I needed to put more cream on my back, but I was too absorbed in trying to whittle my research proposal down to eighty thousand words.

'G'day. Fancy a mojito?'

I didn't just jump metaphorically, I jack-knifed, so that my laptop got covered in sand. I scrambled to put my bikini top back on.

'Lorna told me I'd find you here. Look, if it's not convenient, we can meet up later.'

'No, yes, mojito.' I stood up, trembling like a rabbit, flicking sand from my towel thoughtlessly into David's face.

Sitting upright in the bar, I was taking tiny sips of my mojito every few seconds to avoid having to say anything. David was looking at me with that comfortable smile which I remembered so well. 'Bruce sends his regards. He and I know you two didn't get on, but he's been very helpful in preparing me for this trip.'

I didn't know what to say. I looked at David, then sharply averted my eyes, realising that I'd been staring.

'I've read your story. It's brilliantly written and scores ten out of ten for honesty.'

That really panicked me. My relationship with David may have been confused, but I'd tried to put down what had happened as truthfully as possible.

That meant that my feelings had been exposed as nakedly as my clumsy performances. I now wished I'd left those bits out, but how could I have known that I would ever meet him again? And how could I know that the bitch Rachel would convince me to give her permission to put my story out so that the whole world could watch it while munching their popcorn? 'I'm sorry,' I murmured. Sorry was a word I hated using.

'What for?'

'For those things I wrote about you, about us.'

'Don't be. It's part of your story, so you rightly put it in. Don't worry, I can make it easy for you.' His smile was even more encouraging, but I had to look away. 'You see, in this movie, I'm Bruce. You didn't like Bruce, we both know that, so it wasn't your fault that things went wrong with him. That caused you to have your accident.'

'Did it?'

'Are you still unsure what happened? With Bruce's help, I've been able to fill in some of the gaps. Will you take a walk along the beach with me?'

. . . .

I didn't like it at all. I was shit-scared David was going to hold my hand. Here we were, recreating the walk leading up to that horrible moment when I'd grabbed David by the crotch. I was relieved when we passed the point where I'd committed my *faux pas*. We reached the end of the beach. After clambering over some rocks, I found myself in a narrow bay. Looking between low cliffs and past the mouth to the open sea, I could just see a neighbouring island no more than a couple of miles away. I knew I'd been in this place before. The feeling was elusive, as though from a vaguely remembered dream from long ago. It felt pleasant, but unnerving. Something had corrupted the paradise, but I couldn't tell what it was.

David was pointing to our right. 'See that low cliff up there? That's where Bruce said he spotted you. He had followed you here, you see. Let's go up and have a look.'

It didn't take long. The distance was short and the cliff no more than thirty feet high. I stared out over the strait between the two islands. A steady breeze was blowing from our left. The sea and the sky looked blue, too blue. Something was wrong. I felt unsteady. My head was starting to swim, and I had the horrible feeling that I might be lifted up by the wind and blown out to sea. I felt I had lost control of my actions. Looking down towards the sea made me dizzy. I grabbed David by the hand.

'Take me back, I'm tired.' I wasn't tired, it was something else.

David let go of my hand and started guiding me by the shoulder, back down the path. 'No worries. I know for certain now. You've been here before.'

....

David had joined me for one of my regular meetings with Neil. I'd told Neil that I still didn't know what had happened just before, during, and after my accident, but that David had said he knew how I'd ended up in the sea. Definitely how, not so conclusively why.

David started by telling Neil what he knew. 'Bruce has told me that he had climbed up the cliff and had got quite close to Athena. He saw her pull off her blouse and then step out of her jeans and dive into the sea.'

Neil nodded slowly. 'How about this, then? Athena had had all these problems with David. She was depressed and wanted to be alone. David followed her, so she became upset and confused. Distraught, she dived into the sea. Could that be what happened, Athena?'

I stood up, ready to run away. I was staring hard at David, who was smiling at me encouragingly.

I sat down abruptly. 'It'll have to do. Go with it.' I couldn't believe I had dived from that great height just to get away from Bruce, who'd now become David. I know how to look after myself. Had I been depressed after my failure with David? Yes, but anticipation of arriving in West Papua and my excitement over my future contact with Dollen had more than cancelled that out. I decided I would never know the reason, and Neil's proposal was as good as any.

....

So, how have I spent my day? Snogging David. So, not the whole day, and not all snogging. But I had to perform with my love interest, as they say. They'd readily agreed not to put the incident where I'd grabbed David by the crotch into the script, but we'd had to work hard to get the cringe cabin scene taken out. It looked like Neil was beginning to defer to Tracey, but David backed me up. Then Becks, my stunt double, offered to stand in for me, ogling David as she did so, the saucy cow. David wasn't having it and suggested instead that we have more kissing on the beach, at the end of which I would slap him hard on the cheek to indicate that it hadn't gone well. We needed several takes, the first because I stuck my tongue out at Becks over David's shoulder. The second was because I was meant to take a swipe at him and miss. I didn't miss. I caught him on the cheek with the flat of my hand. It wasn't that David's uniquely Australian expletive was there for all to hear, before Tracey could say 'Cut.' That could be edited out. Rather it was because David burst out laughing while I was in the act of stumbling, having swung myself off my feet.

Although we had a good laugh, I was finding the physical intimacy yucky. Tracey stopped the shoot for a few minutes and took me to one side. 'What you're experiencing is entirely normal. I see it all the time. I know you can act; you were good in the screen test and you've performed well out here. It's not David you're kissing, you're not making any commitment to him, nor he to you. You're performing professionally with an actor who's playing the part of a guy called David.'

It worked. It made me want to act like the pro I'd become.

Much as I would have liked to see Becks split her face open, it obviously wasn't safe for her to dive off the cliff in the same spot as I'd done. A similar looking location had been found where they'd surveyed the water to make sure there weren't any meat-slicers lurking beneath. They filmed me looking moodily out over the strait then turning to see David approach. I stood up, stripped down to my bra and panties, then positioned myself ready to dive. Then they shot Becks from a boat below actually doing so. They'd already filmed her swimming underwater close to some sharp coral. No one knew what had ripped my face open, but coral seemed a good bet. They filmed David looking distraught and then running back to get help.

Lorna and Tracey had warned me that from now on I would have to spend an hour and a half each day being made up, and half an hour at the end of shooting being made down. I liked Libby, the makeup artist. Her fingers moving lightly across my face made my body tingle while I thought of Ekapamne. I remembered what I looked like when Yaku had shown me my face in her rusty mirror. So when Libby had finished with me and I could see my reflection, I cried out, 'Bitch no, that's not how I looked. That's disgusting.' I'd shouted so loudly that Tracey and Lorna came to join us, accompanied by a swarthy man who I took to be an Indonesian. He seemed vaguely familiar, and then I realised that he was the man who'd ferried me back to Sundabang when I was delirious with malaria and hepatitis and was in danger of losing my leg.

'This is Bok,' said Tracey. 'He and his brother

Duk pulled you out of the sea. By all accounts, they saved your life, because you were being swept away in a tidal race in shark-infested waters. You don't know what you looked like then, but Bok does. Remember, you only saw yourself after Umpanu had carried out several operations. You looked very different then from when Bok saved you. We're now going to be shooting the rescue scene. Becks will stand in for you for the long shot as Bok and Duk fish you out of the water. But it's your face we'll shoot from the boat, so at last you can do some swimming. After that we'll shoot you lying on your back while Bok performs first aid.'

'Why wasn't I told about this? I haven't been given a script.'

'That's because you don't have any lines today.' Lorna whispered something to Tracey, who looked shocked. 'I'm sorry, we seem to have slipped up. You should still have received the script, because you're very much in the action.'

I watched while Becks, whose face Libby had also distorted to look like mine, rose spluttering from beneath the waves. Then it was my turn. Libby had given me a bag of beetroot juice which I had to bite on to make it look as though blood was pouring from my mouth. For Bok and Duk pulling me from the sea, Becks did the longer shots and I did the close-ups. Then it was all me.

Bok's first aid was icky. Tracey asked me to scream and squirm, but I didn't need much telling. I repeatedly gagged as Bok stuck strips of shark's liver near my mouth. Listening to Tracey cooing,

'That's good, that's very good,' made me want to sit up and throw the shit at her.

'Cut! That's it for the day. Tomorrow we'll shoot the scene with the yacht and Athena in the water. We're doing it here on Sundabang rather than on Papua. Becks, that gash on your foot shows every sign of turning septic. We need to get you to the medical post. Athena, that means you'll have to do the scene where you get attacked by the people on the yacht by yourself. Happy with that?'

'Oh yes.' I couldn't help throwing gloaty shade at Becks. Later that evening, I went to find Bok and Duk. We couldn't converse in English or Indonesian, so we used Walukek. Our words were stilted, so I threw my arms around Bok and hugged him. Then I did the same with Duk.

....

I was sitting on one of the few bar stools which hadn't got a tear in it, having a farewell drink with David. The lights were harsh and the smell of booze from previous nights staled the air.

He gave me his confident smile. 'Are we friends?'

'Of course.' Tonight, I felt more at ease with him. We both finally knew we would never be more than friends.

'So, what's stirring the waters in Cambridge?'

It took me several seconds to realise that he wasn't referring to the River Cam. I assumed he was asking what the hot topics of debate were. I stared at him. 'Whether we've already entered the Anthropocene Period.'

'Is that part of your astrophysics studies?'

'Nothing to do with it. It comes under the subject of chronostratigraphy.'

David leant back and smiled. 'Of course it does. I think you'd better explain that one.'

I tried to think of something he could relate to. 'Jurassic? Triassic?'

He closed his eyes and nodded. 'Ah, the dinosaurs.'

'Those are examples of periods. They're a subdivision of eons at the highest level and then eras. Below periods, we have epochs, and finally ages, the lowest sub-division.'

'So why do we talk about the age of the dinosaurs?'

'You shouldn't, it's wrong.'

'Is there any subject you don't know about?'

What a peculiar question, I thought. Of course there are things I know nothing about.

'So this anthropopo… what did you say it was?'

'Anthropocene. It's defined by humans' impact on the planet, including geological strata.'

'You're not saying we're having an effect on the rocks?'

'I am saying that. We're laying down huge deposits of plastic and concrete. It's not just on land. Fossil fuels and artificial fertilisers are changing the chemistry of the waters and air at a rapidly increasing rate. When we're long gone, the geological evidence of our brief time on earth will be there in layers of sediment. Thirty-eight percent of the land surface is used for agriculture and a further three percent is urban. Both are rising. Only four percent of mammals are wild, the rest have been modified to feed or serve us. The word unsustainable doesn't do it justice.'

David leaned back. 'So the planet's fucked?'

'Not the planet. We are. The planet's survived much worse in the past. It's we who will face extinction. Our bodies are too fragile to resist the coming trauma, and our interdependence on technology and each other is too complex to withstand even minor shocks. Once the interlinking chains are broken, society will collapse.

'Back to the planet. Moves from one geological period to another have often been marked by mass extinction events. This transition will be no different, but unlike asteroids hitting the earth or prolonged volcanic activity, we will have been the cause. The annihilation is already underway. We're destroying species at a thousand times the natural rate of extinction.'

Lorna came up to us looking worried. 'Sorry to disturb. Tracey would like to see you now in the lounge, Athena.'

David stood up. 'This is goodbye, then. I'm leaving before dawn. I'll never forget you, Athena. You'll always be very special to me.' I moved to kiss him on the cheek and was met by his outstretched hand. We both laughed and I won, so we held each other in a brief hug.

I felt disorientated as I entered the lounge, so it took me a minute or two to realise that Tracey was looking as though she'd just been trolled by half the world.

'Sit down, Athena, there's been a development. We've got one more day's shooting here on Sundabang and then we move on to West Papua. As I expect you know, I've had part of my team staying near the Walukek village for the past fortnight. They've been selecting and preparing the tribal actors and extras, including costume design for those men who are going to be playing the part of Suamu warriors, the ones who abducted you.'

That jolted me back from thinking about David. I wondered how they'd be coaching Ekapamne.

'Rachel's safely back from her stay with the Suamu. She's sent a message via a runner. She's got the wild shots which she wanted, although she's still frustrated that she hasn't got a battle scene. The problem is this. Somehow, the Suamu have got to hear that Golgola's about to be staying with the Walukek. Rachel doesn't know how they've found out.'

I clicked my fingers. 'Bili, she's been with Rachel. She's either blurted it out by accident, or deliberately. She's a Suamu.'

'That's not all,' Tracey was saying. 'The Suamu have had a disastrous time since you were there. Many of them died of dysentery last year and a few months ago a landslide following a cyclone destroyed part of the village. Again, there was loss of life.'

'And the Walukek? Were they affected?' I was thinking of Ekapamne.

'Not so much. But the point is that Rachel has

found out that the Suamu are blaming you for their disasters. It's lucky for Rachel that they don't seem to have held her responsible in any way for you or your escape two years ago.'

'So, the problem is?'

'You, your safety.'

I snorted. 'That's bollocks. Where's the filming going to be taking place?'

'In the Walukek village and in the forest nearby. Look, Athena, we can delay going there until I've laid on an armed guard. Lorna's contacting the authorities in Jakarta. Remember, Rachel's got contacts high up in the Indonesian government.'

'If I hear any more about Rachel's contacts, I'll walk off this set. If you delay now, your budget and most likely the whole movie will be jeopardised.' I then gave Tracey a detailed explanation of the physics of momentum, which I thought she'd find useful.

She shook her head doubtfully at me. 'Rachel warned me about you. She said that you'd be difficult to work with, stubborn, and opinionated. But she also said you were positive and had more guts than anyone she'd ever met.'

I ignored all that froth. Instead, I said, 'Think what you've got to complete: a gobsmacking story, mine, a fascinating record of a way of life which is about to disappear for ever, and a relationship between two warring tribes which is almost certainly unique in the world. My part has got to end in two months' time, and that includes doing the narration in London. No ifs, no buts, it's in my fucking contract. So, no delay.' I stood up. Since she didn't say any more, I walked towards the door.

'Athena?' I turned and gave her my hard stare. 'Thank you.' She looked as if she might say more, but any further discussion would have been futile. I'd made my decision, so I left the room.

....

It was our last day on Sundabang. I was sitting on my little balcony looking out over the water. A yacht glided round the headland and entered the small bay, slowing all the time. I watched a woman at the stern operating the wheel, a man at the front looking as though he had his hands on an anchor, and a second woman in sunglasses and a yachting cap standing statuesquely towards the rear, surveying the scene. The boat stopped and the anchor was thrown overboard. When Tracey shouted, 'Action!' I stood up, stepped out of my smock, crouched down, and swung my legs under a rail. Then I slid feet first into the water. I swam up to the yacht. There were two shots, one of me entering the water, the other swimming up to the yacht.

'Hi.'

The women turned towards me looking startled. One was played by Lorna, the other by Jessica, my *ersatz* mother, heavily made up to disguise her.

'Help!'

Lorna started screaming, rhythmically, hysterically. The owner of the yacht, a man, picked up a boat hook and started thrusting it towards my face. Tracey had told me to stay still, but to put up my arms as though I was fending the thing off. It wasn't easy to hold my position while treading water, but I knew that if I moved sideways, the man might hit me, and two mutilations of the face is enough for one lifetime. A bite on another of Libby's beetroot bags made it look as though he'd hit me and I was spurting blood. Tracey shouted, 'Cut'! I cried out, 'Fucking headbusta,' but it didn't matter. All that was left was to shoot Jessica pretending to vomit over the side, and a shot of the yacht powering out of the bay.

They say that supermodels fall in love with their photographers. I'm not a supermodel, but I do find Ollie, the cameraman, fit. I'm a disciplined professional, so I can enter my acting bubble without any distractions. It's like when I'm working on a new formula; nothing else exists. But when the filming's over for the day, I find myself wanting to know where Ollie is. He's got his own clique of mates within the crew, but when he's not talking to them, I notice his eyes straying towards me. He hasn't come on to me yet. It's still a bit too close to David's departure for me to want to make my own move. Sometime, maybe.

....

The nearer I got to the Walukek village, the more hyper I became. The humidity and my breathing were both off the scale. I was bummed when they took me to the camp where the film crew were living rather than to the tribal village. I wasn't doing any acting for the rest of the day, but they wanted me to settle into my tent. I had it to myself, but it was hardly glamping. Then I was expected to work with Neil on some new part of the script. I said I wanted to go and meet my friends in the tribal village.

Lorna tried to stop me. 'We have a rule here that none of the crew are allowed to visit the village without permission and, even then, there has to be a very good reason.'

The crew? Who did she think I was? I thought of telling her that they were my friends there; I'd lived, loved, and suffered with them. But I thought it was easier just to ignore her and wander off when no one was looking.

Yaku welcomed me and even the normally stern Umpanu managed half a smile. Ekapamne was beside me before I saw her coming. We hugged, we high-fived, we punched each other, and screamed, 'Lua, lua, lua' so loudly that half the village came out to join us, even some of the warriors. She kept touching my face, her fingers hovering over my mouth. I was ready to bring the whole fucking movie to a halt if they'd found someone else to play the part of Ekapamne, but they hadn't. We would be filming together, my brave Ekapamne, speaking, touching, and standing shoulder to shoulder with me as the Suamu warriors closed in.

It felt good to be back in my Walukek clobber. I wore it proudly, even when we weren't filming. It made me feel exotic again and distinguished me from the crew in their western scruffs. Conversing with the Walukek in their own language impressed everyone. I'd made it clear to Tracey, Lorna, and now Rachel, that I wasn't bound by their rules and could pass as I pleased between the Walukek village and Tent City. Sometimes I had my meals in one, at other times the other. I felt relaxed in both and proud that I was the only person who fully bridged both communities.

Rachel told me about the Suamus' disasters. 'Remember when we first met in the Suamu village? I said you could be in danger then. Just as they praised you for their small victory over the Walukek, things could turn sour with Golgola if they had a setback? It's exactly as I'd predicted.'

Was she expecting me to tell her how fucking wonderful she was? I remained silent.

'They do blame you for what happened last year. What's more, they've found out that you're here. But don't worry, I'm laying on some extra security. Just don't go wandering off into the forest, and when you do go into the Walukek village, stay near the centre.'

I'd had enough. I didn't need a second mother. I stood up. 'Thank you,' I said, after giving her a long cold stare.

Lying motionless as Umpanu pretended to operate on my face wasn't as yucky as it'd been with Bok, but it was just as tedious, especially as it followed an hour and a half being made up by Libby. Rachel kept whinging that they didn't have any footage of the actual fighting between the Walukek and the Suamu, but I ignored her and threw myself into my part, first the feast and then the dancing. The whole crew laughed at the way I pretended to pick up a rock, burn my hand, and drop it onto my foot. They loved the faces I made when I had to eat grubs and beetles. Each scene took only two takes. Tracey had asked me if I would be able to speak intelligibly with the muffled voice I'd had when I was out in Papua. She'd said it wouldn't be easy, but I should give it a go. If it didn't work, I should revert to my normal voice, and they would adjust it in the studio later. Tracey says I've slayed it. I hope Ollie's impressed too, but when he's working, he's utterly focused.

The event which would make the greatest demands on my acting skills was the one where the four Suamu warriors surrounded us in the fields and then abducted me. I would have to strike a perfect balance between terror and spunky defiance. The wardrobe team had spent a long time designing costumes so that four Walukek warriors looked like Suamu. One of them was Ekapamne's husband. Although the action wasn't dangerous enough to need stunt doubles, Tracey still insisted that the warriors had blunted spears, and that we did slow-motion actions before the shooting began. After my past experiences, it wasn't surprising that I'd become jumpy when anyone waved anything towards my face. Tracey said it was acceptable that I should flinch, because it balanced my natural desire to be defiant. But I've never shown weakness in the face of aggression, so wincing was cringe to me.

We'd got to the bit where one of the warriors had taken a swipe at Ekapamne with the side of his spear, so that she stumbled. I screamed at her to run. The other women, who'd held back, turned and fled, taking Ekapamne with them. I thought we'd all done it well, but Tracey wanted another take.

Everything had been reset, ready to roll again, when we became aware of a commotion coming from the Walukek village half a mile away. We all paused to listen, wondering what it meant. It was the four Walukek warriors dressed as Suamu who told me, and I relayed it to the crew.

'The Suamu are attacking down in the valley. This is for real.'

Everyone was rooted, listening to shouts and screams coming from ahead. The four warriors weren't waiting. They were rushing towards the village, having dropped their spears. Their weapons for filming were blunt, so they had to go and arm themselves properly. Even more importantly, they were dressed as Suamu warriors, so would be in as much danger from the Walukek as from the Suamu, until they changed their clobber.

I'd expected Tracey to order everyone to hold fast or get back to Tent City, but she never got the chance. Led by Ollie, her team were sprinting in the direction of the fighting: cameraman, focus puller, boom operator, producer, director, everyone except Ekapamne, the other Walukek women, and me. Rachel and Tracey had banged on for so long that the biggest flaw in the movie was the failure to get action shots of a real fight. So when the moment came, it was instinctive that everyone would leap, literally leap, at the opportunity. I sprinted after them.

But I didn't follow them far. Rachel had warned me that the Suamu were furious with Golgola, so I guessed that if I ran up to the film crew, she would make shit that I hadn't retreated. So I veered off to the left to avoid them, even though that was in the direction of Suamu territory.

I remembered the topography quite well. The slope started to drop away more steeply where the forest gave way to open grassland, except in two places. There, fingers of land half a mile apart, jutted out over the valley. The film crew had set up on the right-hand spur, a good choice, because it gave a hundred-and-eighty-degree view of the scene below. I took the left-hand point. I too could look out ahead and to my right, although the view to my left was restricted by trees close by.

I lay down on my tummy. I was well camouflaged by my Walukek bark skirt and bib, and my dark skin. The battle scene below seemed chaotic. There didn't appear to be any co-ordinated tactics on either side. I could recognise the two tribes from their different coloured feathers. The Walukek were moving most of the time from the right and the Suamu from the left. Individuals rushed at each other, feinted, retreated, pursued, and broke off. I could see spears and bows, but it was only possible at that distance to detect arrows from the movements of the archers.

I was jolted unpleasantly when I noticed a Walukek fall. I watched in horror as his opponent closed in on him and finished him off with his spear. It was then that I thought of Ekapamne's husband. Fearful and disgusted, I realised that this balletic mêlée was deadly, and that its purpose was for men to kill each other.

The Suamu seemed to have the greater numbers, and more were coming in from the left. Beyond where the grassland fell away, low scrub bracketed either side of the river. A group of about fifteen Suamu were creeping through the bushes on the far side, I guessed so that they could cross and outflank the Walukek on my right. A vague thought flashed through my mind that they could just as easily storm Tent City or attack the tribal village. Were they looking for Golgola?

I froze. Another group of nine Suamu emerged from the trees to my left. They were heading for the higher part of the grassy slope ahead of me. If they maintained their course, they would pass less than a hundred metres from where I lay. They might not see me, provided I remained still. But they were heading straight towards the camera crew, who would be concentrating so hard on filming the fighting that they might not spot them. What were the chances that the Suamu had any interest in anything other than fighting the Walukek? I hadn't a clue, but I wasn't taking any chances. I needed to warn the crew. I ran across the spur which overlooked the valley, then tumbled down the slope on the far side. The ground was now almost flat ahead of me, and then it climbed steadily up to where the crew were filming. The warriors must have seen me the moment I'd moved, but now for perhaps a minute I was out of their line of sight. Once out in the open, I had no time to turn round to see what they were doing but continued my sprint towards the second spur. I'd now reached the position of greatest danger, because my progress would be slowed by having to climb up the slope. It wasn't high, barely thirty feet, but it was covered in small boulders. Before I started to clamber up the slope, I turned to see where the Suamu were and whether they were pursuing me or passing to my left.

That was my first mistake. I saw instantly that they weren't looking at me, but rather had their sights on the Walukek below. They must have seen me, but they wouldn't be thinking of Golgola or recognise her from behind. One lone Walukek woman was probably of no interest to them. Or was she? Rachel had told me long ago that women were often seized and abducted.

The warriors were no longer straight behind me. I looked left and saw them little more than fifty metres away. Just as I was about to turn and start to climb up towards the camera crew, I saw one of the warriors pointing at me. The others stopped dead in their tracks. It was then that I realised I'd been recognised. I was no longer a Walukek woman, nor even Athena the movie star. I was Golgola, facing the people I'd betrayed.

I could tell they were dithering. Their orders, assuming they had any, were probably to fight the Walukek in the valley. But they would also know that Golgola was an important prize, dead or alive. Dead or alive? The thought made me want to shit myself. If dead, they would soon finish me off. I would only have seconds more to live, before the arrows got me. If alive? All the terrors I'd faced that night in the Suamu village two years ago surged into my mind: gang rape, torture, ritual execution. Could Golgola still exercise a hold over them? Should I march towards them swearing at them in my best vernacular, imitating Adolf Hitler or doing the *haka*? Might they then turn and run when faced with my awesome power? Would I be a coward if I turned away? I would never know.

The gunshot which rang out made me jump with fright and then stagger to regain my balance. I hadn't a clue where it'd come from. There seemed to be more than one, but it was hard to tell, as it had echoed around the valley. My instincts were to turn and start climbing up the slope towards the camera crew. But before I could do so, I became mesmerised by what was happening below me on my left. The group of Suamu warriors nearby were spinning round in confusion, some looking down towards the valley, others looking as though they might be urging their comrades to run up towards me. Four of them broke away and were heading straight for me. Another shot rang out, and I saw a vicious spit where a bullet had ripped into the turf between me and the men. They paused and then started to run towards me again. I noticed with horror that one of them had an arrow slung in his bow, ready to shoot. I backed away, holding my arms in front of my chest and my hands spread out to protect my face. Then I turned to meet the slope towards the camera crew above. I felt the terror of knowing that the arrow might enter my back at any moment. Even if he didn't shoot, they would soon be on me. I ignored the next gunshot but turned around again when I heard screaming close behind me. The warrior who'd held the bow was clutching his leg while two of the others tried to hold him upright. Another shot hit a boulder and sang out to my left. Transfixed, I watched the men turn and start to hobble and run down towards the valley. I was shaking.

'Athena!' Rachel was gazing down. An Indonesian man I'd barely noticed before stood beside her holding a rifle. Lorna and Ollie were coming down the slope towards me. My knees gave way and I fell onto the grass, sobbing.

PART X

The gunshots which rang out changed their lives for ever. Never again would two tribes in Papua New Guinea fight each other by the old methods, ritualistically, using bows, arrows, and spears. All trust between the Suamu and the Walukek had been shattered. But Awhina had been saved.

Umpanu's stern face was cracked with fury. His normally calm surgeon's hands were clenched. He wanted them all to leave immediately. Awhina knew she'd been the cause of his anger. Although Rachel and Tracey didn't directly accuse her, Rachel had told her curtly that they were being thrown out. 'We've had to negotiate hard to delay our departure until the morning. That's the best we could get. All those scenes with you and the Suamu, they'll never happen now, gone for ever.'

Awhina meandered listlessly around Tent City in the rain. No one wanted to look at her. Her misery was compounded by the realisation that Rachel had saved her life. No one would care that Awhina's own motive had been to save theirs. Awhina had never liked expressing gratitude to anyone. It could only smoulder inside her as guilt. All that was left for her now was to see Ekapamne one last time. She came across her easily enough but was shocked to find her friend wary and frightened. She knew that any detailed explanation would be futile. For one thing, she didn't know exactly what had happened. She wanted to hug Ekapamne but was sure the gesture would be rebuffed. Awhina stood up, ready to go. Realising that a dignified exit was all she could hope for, she was wondering whether to say any more or just back away.

Yaku entered looking serious but not hostile. She motioned for Awhina to squat down again and then did so herself.

'Why have you brought guns?'

'I didn't know there was a gun. I don't like guns.'

'We should never have allowed you to come here.'

'I'm sorry.'

Yaku said something Awhina didn't understand. Partly to gain time, and partly because she was genuinely struggling with a language which she'd only spoken for a few months in her life, Awhina asked for Bili to be brought in to translate. Ekapamne went to fetch her.

Yaku was looking sadly at Awhina. 'You did not need guns. We do not need them, so why should you? You were not in any danger.'

It wouldn't be much of a justification, but

Awhina went for it. She told Yaku how Rachel had found out that the Suamu knew that Golgola would soon be coming to the Walukek village. Not only had Golgola run away without warning, but the tribe had experienced a succession of disasters after she'd left. They'd blamed Golgola. Knowing that the Suamu might want to capture or kill Golgola, Rachel had tried to get the government to provide protection for her but had failed. She must have hired a man locally to protect her. Awhina hadn't been told that. She gave Yaku one of her long stares but tried to soften it. 'I owe everything to you and Umpanu. You saved my life. Everyone has been so kind to me. Now guns have come here, and our film has been ruined. Without those scenes of when I was with the Suamu, my story means nothing.'

Yaku was staring straight ahead. 'It was not your fault that the Suamu captured you out in the fields. You did well to escape from them, and you nearly died doing so.'

She turned to Bili. 'How did the Suamu know that Golgola was coming here?'

Bili shook her head sadly. 'I told them. It was a mistake.' She started to cry.

Yaku turned to Awhina, who for the first time saw compassion in the older woman's face. 'So many mistakes. So many, but none of them yours. I see now how you have suffered. You have faced death so many times. It is not right for a woman. I will speak to my husband. Come.'

Yaku and Awhina squatted in front of Umpanu. He looked unforgiving, but at least he seemed prepared to listen. He never interrupted while Yaku spoke slowly for a long time. Awhina could understand less than half of what she was saying. When at last she'd finished, Umpanu sighed and scratched his head. Awhina couldn't understand his first words, which were to Yaku. Then he turned to Awhina without softening his demeanour. He addressed her in broken English.

'Three times. Three times you near die. Three times you show brave. When Bok brought you me, you near dead. You show me. You show me saving you good, right thing to do.' Awhina looked anxiously at Yaku, who gave her a weak smile.

There was a long silence before he spoke again. But crucial words could not be understood between them in either language. Bili was no longer with them to translate. He tried again, this time in Walukek. 'You need better.'

'Deserve better?' Awhina offered, but the words still weren't understood.

There was a frustrated silence and another long pause. 'What would you like?' Umpanu suddenly asked in Walukek.

Awhina seized her opportunity. She spoke in a mixture of Walukek and English. 'You say I have been brave. I love you and the Walukek people. I love being here. You were brave too when you brought me here and allowed me to live with you. You were brave when you allowed me to tell my story. Now my story is broken. Without filming what happened to me when I was with the Suamu, I am incomplete.' That word could not be understood. Awhina tried again. 'Without the Suamu, my story is no good. I will go home after wasting nearly a year of my life. I have thrown it away,' she added for clarity.

There was another long pause. After some time, Yaku said a couple of words which Umpanu seemed to ignore. Eventually he looked straight at Awhina and spoke in English. 'You can stay again.'

She wasn't exactly sure what that meant. 'And film?'

'Yes.'

Her emotions were churning in a tangle of surprise, disbelief, relief, love. She stayed motionless just long enough for tears to fill her eyes. She stood up and embraced first Umpanu and then Yaku. She left them and started to walk towards Tent City. Then she took a long detour through the forest, gathering her thoughts.

. . . .

Awhina wondered why no one had asked her why she'd walked out in front of a group of Suamu warriors. She decided she wasn't going to tell them. Rachel, Tracey, and the others had made it clear that they were annoyed with her. If reasons and logic didn't matter to them, that was their problem, not hers.

She walked into the kitchen tent and was served a plate of curry, rice, and what looked like spinach. She entered the dining tent, only looking out of the corners of her eyes to see where Rachel and Tracey were sitting. She took a place as far away from them as possible, next to the camera crew. Ollie glanced at her without smiling. No one spoke to her. They continued with a conversation they were having about football back home. They'd started their meal long before she had, so they soon got up and left. Awhina's mouth was so dry that she was finding it difficult to eat.

Rachel came up to her, followed by Tracey. 'We'll be leaving at 9.30. The porters will be here at 8.30. Make sure your things are fully packed and ready by then. We can talk on the journey home.' Her tone was cold.

Awhina waited until they had nearly reached the flaps of the tent. 'I'm staying.'

Rachel turned and walked back to Awhina's table. She looked down contemptuously at her. 'You can't stay. You'd be in breach of contract. We've still got the narration to film. And your escape from the Suamu. We were going to shoot that in the forest near here. We can't anymore. Now we've got to find another location and different actors. I thought you were in a rush to get home to your PhD?'

'What are you planning to do here?' Tracey asked, less scornfully than Rachel.

'I'll be filming.'

Rachel was sarcastic. 'What with? Taking selfies?'

'No, I'll have a film crew.'

Awhina had never heard Rachel swear before. 'Don't be so fucking ridiculous.'

Awhina stood up. 'Would you like to hear it from Umpanu yourself, or shall I come with you? No one's leaving in the morning. You can shoot the rest of the fucking movie here. I've arranged it. You'd better let your crew know.'

PART XI

TWO YEAS LATER

'Athena?' It was a man's voice, coming from my right, near the cheese stall.

It happens quite often, and when it does, I don't mind. Mostly, strangers address me as Golgola. That's because *Golgola* was the name of the film, and they recognise me as having played the part. They say how much they enjoyed it and usually ask for my autograph. But occasionally, someone will remember the name of the narrator, Athena Fernandez. That's fine too. It's a world I've left behind, but I don't object to being reminded of it briefly. I'd rather be acknowledged as a scientist, but fame comes to people for the wrong reasons.

I'd come by train from Cambridge to London and was walking through Borough Market taking in the smells of coffee, frying fish, and curry. I was trying to decide between samosas and some intriguing looking savoury pastries being offered by an Afghan woman. As soon as I heard "Athena", I slowed without looking round, as I always do when my name is called. The market was crowded, so there were people close to me on all sides. I stopped.

'Athena, hi.' Before me stood Ollie, looking tanned. He was wearing a bronze overshirt, loose black joggers, and a gold chain. 'It's great to see you. Have you eaten?'

We decided that conversation would be easier in a pub.

He shook his head as though disbelieving he was really with me. 'You know, working with you on *Golgola* was one of the highlights of my career. Have you done any more acting? Your talent is out there for all to see.'

'It's not my passion.'

'How about your book? I know Rachel was keen to get it published at the same time as the movie. Mutual promotion, each boosting interest in the other?'

'I'd only written forty thousand words. That was my story, and they based the movie on that. Any extension of it would simply have been padding.' A waiter came with our food, mine a lasagne, his steak and chips. 'Anyhow, I didn't have the time. I needed to crack on with my PhD course.'

'Ah yes, I remember now; you're an astronomer.'

'Astrophysicist.'

'Sounds impressive. So is your course full-time?'

'It is for most people, but I work on other projects not always related to my thesis. I've just got back from Canada.'

Six months earlier, Pheen Khodan had sent me a message. 'Professor Dollen would like to put you forward as a keynote speaker at the International Conference on Interdisciplinary Physics in Toronto. He wants you to present your paper on Quantum Chromodynamics. He says the committee has virtually agreed to give you a ninety-minute slot, but the application has to come from you. Time is very short. Please respond by return.'

It was exciting. That my paper had gained such recognition was one thing, but the chance to persuade any doubters in person was something else. I've never been scared of public speaking; in fact, I'm good at it. Being in full control of my subject gives me total confidence and a feeling of power. But there was a problem. Standing in front of a couple of hundred top scientists from around the world wouldn't faze me. But meeting them before and afterwards, chatting in ones and twos, making small talk, no, I couldn't do it.

I replied, 'Please thank Professor Dollen, but my other commitments force me to decline.' I was pleased that I'd asserted my independence.

Within twenty minutes, the man himself had come on the phone. 'Do you want to participate in scientific advancement or don't you? I'm fed up with your excuses. I believe you have a significant contribution to make, but if you hide behind your screen all the time, people will simply ignore you, including me.'

That shocked me. I found my hands trembling. The silence which followed was freaking me out.

'I need an answer, Athena, and I need it now. I'm prepared to invest in you if you behave like an adult.'

'I'll come.' I hoped my voice hadn't sounded like a whimper.

He softened. 'I'm pleased. You've made the right call. I'll get Pheen to send you the forms right away. If you have any problems, let her know. I'll help you if necessary. And Athena? Don't forget I'll be there at the conference, promoting you and supporting you.'

He'd rung off before he could hear my tearful, 'Thank you.'

....

I didn't tell Ollie all of that. Instead, I said, 'The applause lasted several minutes. I'd walked out from behind the lectern in that vast hall in Toronto. Dollen had joined me on stage, leading the applause with his hands in front of his face. That evening was more exhausting than giving my speech. People were queuing up to ask questions. But it wasn't their praise I valued, it was the knowledge that my ground-breaking theory had been understood. That is the world I must inhabit. So now you can see why I don't want to do any more movies.'

Ollie nodded slowly. 'Yes, I can see that. But you will come to the award ceremony, won't you?'

'What award ceremony?'

'You're joking? Haven't you been told? The BAFTAs. *Golgola*'s just been nominated for a BAFTA. Outstanding British Film. I can't believe you didn't know.'

'That must be why Rachel's been sending me phone and voice messages for the past week. I haven't had time to deal with them.'

'So now you know. But with those fabulous reviews and high viewing figures, you must have thought about the possibility?'

'Nope.'

'But you know what the BAFTAs are?'

'Of course I do. British Academy of Film and Television Awards. I've got to go now.'

'It's on May 18th at the Royal Albert Hall. See you then.'

I didn't tell him I had no intention of being there.

....

Rachel fucking Atkinson, MBE. Why do you have to haunt me? And why do I think that I dislike you more than I do. Right, bitch, I told myself, I'm going to spend one hour on you, no more, and I'm going to analyse my relationship with you scientifically, without emotion.

Suamu village, first impressions. MBE on her luggage label. Attention-seeker. Establishment arse-licker. 'It's not what you know, etc.' Same with her poncey club in London. Annoying? Yes. Important? No. Following me around in the village. Nosey, intrusive. Yes, but it was only later that I discovered her reasons. If it hadn't been for Rachel, I would never have found out about the cult of Golgola, nor how much danger it put me in.

Helping me escape from the Suamu. She didn't

do a lot, but then there wasn't much more she could do.

Staying with me when I was high-key ill and likely to die. Accompanying me from the Walukek village to Sundabang, Sulawesi, Jakarta, and London. That must have cost her a lot in time, and even more in money. And I've never let her know how grateful I am.

Sorting out my insurance. Persuading me to have those operations back home. Crowd funding, persuading Dad to cough up some money, and even putting up some herself. Again, I have never shown gratitude. This is looking more like an analysis of the failings of Athena Fernandez than Rachel Atkinson.

Persuading me to hand over my manuscript and then enticing me to star in the movie. Did she blackmail me? There was blackmail, but it came from me. I'd told her that unless she gave me the leading role, she couldn't use my story. But I passed the screen test. Or did I? Perhaps they couldn't do anything else but give me the part. I'll never know, but at least I was a success in the filming, and the narration. So, nothing wrong with Rachel there. I entered into it with free will.

Telling the gunman to shoot to save my life. Angry with me for preventing them filming the whole battle scene. She was, but that was because I'd never told her that I'd been trying to warn the crew about the Suamu approaching from the left. Later, Tracey, Ollie, and some of the others, had told me that they'd got almost all the shots they'd wanted of the fighting. Close-ups of warriors actually being killed or wounded in real life would never have been allowed to be screened. After I'd persuaded Umpanu that the filming could continue, Rachel had thanked me, more than I'd ever done to her.

Conclusion. My objections to the minor irritations in her character weren't irrational, but they were petty. The two things which dominated all others were her dedication to stay with me when I seemed about to die. And her generosity in arranging and funding the three operations which restored my speech and made my face presentable.

'Rachel? This is Athena. I'm sorry it's taken me all this time to come back to you. Congratulations on the nomination. You deserve to win, and I hope you do. Can I come along and see it, please?'

'I'd be thrilled, Athena. It's your nomination too.'

I didn't give her all the thanks I owed her. I would do that face-to-face on another occasion.

Five days later, Rachel phoned me. 'I want to ask a favour. If we do win, I'd like you to collect the BAFTA on behalf of the whole team. You'd be expected to make a short speech. Would you be happy with that?'

'I've recently given a ninety-minute lecture to a hundred and sixty of the world's leading scientists in Toronto. I slayed it. Yes, I can do it.'

'Good. It's normal for producers or directors to accept awards for films. But your case is so exceptional that I think we can overlook convention. The whole movie's about your experiences, as you wrote them. You're the star and the narrator. That's one hell of a combination. In that sense you *are* the movie. But you'd only be expected to speak for twenty seconds, thirty max. Then I'll take over. Have a look at some acceptance speeches at past BAFTA ceremonies. There's loads on YouTube. Libby's been nominated for a Make-up and Hair Award. I think she might get it. And Athena? Don't expect too much. There's stiff competition, and we haven't been nominated for Best Film Award. Only Outstanding British.'

I watched the YouTube videos, but that didn't mean that I'd follow them.

....

What clothes to wear? I could see from the videos that nearly all the females at the BAFTAs wore gowns. The dress I'd worn at the May Ball with Lily, Adam, and Teddy four years ago would make me look glam. But the T-Rex had thrown it out. Anyhow, I wanted to look different. I thought it would make an impression if I came in my full Walukek clobber, which I'd brought back from Papua. Then I thought no, a star appearing in her movie gear would look naff. I settled on a corduroy miniskirt in burnt orange, a sky-blue frilly blouse, and thigh-length boots. I went to the hairdresser in Cambridge with my photo from four years previously. The girl recreated the look: stylish and wild at the same time.

Rachel had laid on a limo. I got out a second before it had fully stopped, finding myself clutching at the car door to stop myself from falling onto the red carpet. I'd seen videos of stars posing for the cameras. I wanted to get past the photographers who were shouting out 'Golgola' and 'Athena'. Lily had said she would be over on the right. I walked slowly past the assembled people on that side, searching the crowd. I stopped. I couldn't see her.

'Here, Athena, I'm here.' I barged my way through the throng and flung my arms around her. We both squealed. Adam was standing next to Lily with that curious, mocking look of his. I hugged him too, the first time I'd ever touched him.

Rachel was calling urgently from the red carpet, and I realised I had to go. I shouted back to them over my shoulder. 'See you later. After the show? Dinner?'

....

'And the winner is… *Golgola*.'

Five of us stood up and made our way to the stage: me, Rachel, Tracey, Lorna, and Neil. The actor who'd introduced the result, whoever he was, handed me this bronze mask thing on a marble stand, same as all the others. I put it carefully down on the glass table in front of me and leant towards the microphone.

'Great film, but I'm no longer part of all this. I'm an astrophysicist, not an actress. I owe everything to Rachel here, including my life. This is for you, Rachel, catch.'

I didn't exactly throw the BAFTA at her. I left the microphone, and as I walked past her, I thrust the mask into her hands. As I stepped down off the stage, I heard a few gasps and a lone person clapping, who quickly hesitated, then stopped. I could hear my boots clacking as I walked up the aisle, past where I'd been sitting earlier. Rachel was saying something into the microphone, but I wasn't listening. I didn't look back.

AFTERWORD

I do hope that you've enjoyed *Cooee Baby*. I'd be delighted if you would take the time to leave a review on Amazon. Reviews are so important to authors, and do not have to be too long or detailed.

Just a word to say that you liked the book would be very much appreciated.

Charles Moberly

viewauthor.at/CharlesMoberly

ACKNOWLEDGEMENTS

My warmest thanks to Annie Whitehead, historian and novelist, for editing my manuscripts in so many different ways: red-penning my lapses into bad taste and correcting typos, inconsistencies, and other howlers. Annie is always encouraging, but never frightened to point out defects in characterisation or plot.

Cathy Helms of Avalon Graphics continues to come up with vivid and relevant cover designs which make me gasp whenever I first see them. Cathy also converts my manuscripts into a format suitable for Amazon, using Vellum. She handles my sometimes-eccentric layouts with patience and good humour.

My thanks to Helen Hollick, author, for almost everything. She encouraged me to publish in the first place and has supported me with the technology, in which I am sometimes moronically deficient. She developed my blog, which she mostly maintains, except for the simplest tasks which I perform myself. Helen has dug me out of holes over such things as breaches of copyright and has encouraged me and supported me on book tours.

Charles Moberly

Try the Leopard's Mouth

Briony and Tom, both in their twenties, are very different characters. But opposites attract. In business, as in love, they complement each other.

They buy a farm and discover a rare drug. Tom grows it and Briony markets it. At first, they are oblivious of their responsibilities to the land and its people. But gradually they realise that they have been supporting a racist and colonialist regime.

The onset of the Rhodesian – Zimbabwean War of Independence tears at the couple's relationship. Misunderstandings arise from their conflicting personalities and from external pressures. Events pull them apart, but also bind them together.

Try the Leopard's Mouth is a romantic thriller set

in Africa. It is also a historical novel, grounded in real events in the period 1970-80.

The Historical Fiction Company Highly Recommended Award

"Moberly is a mastermind in his craft. Painting an image so vivid of 1970s Rhodesia, later Zimbabwe, with its lush rolling hills, fertile farmland, roaring waters and rich culture that any reader would feel as though they've been dropped into the middle of the African bush. For they are to feel as drawn to it as the characters of the story, regretting when the time comes that they must leave. He has woven a tale of incredible stakes. A country at war with racism embedded into the very foundation of its start. We are thrust into the middle of the goings on and the history of the story delivered is precise, it's harsh in its truth, but it's emotional and sucks the reader in so they are as immersed as the characters are in the plot. A man who just wants to be a farmer is sucked in by the angel he'd never intended to meet and his world of simplicity turns into one of politics, warfare and a drug that can only be fuel to the fire.

"Tom Etheridge, the focal point and narrator of the tale being told, is the kind of character that readers will relate to. He's flawed, but human in every sense of the word. Starting from the mind of a young man looking to find himself in a beautiful land so vastly different from his home back in England he is searching for his purpose. Along the way he makes mistakes, he misunderstands, he reacts at the best of times and doesn't at the worst. Moberly has made Tom's narrative flow so smoothly that it feels as though the reader is listening to an interview of a lifetime. On the edge of their seat, crying with him, laughing at times, but angry at others with a raised fist and a sense of disapproval. Only a well practiced writer could elicit such a response, and Moberly has shown his hand with this novel. He has constructed characters from the middle of their life stories, but during times where decisions lead to either growth or destruction. He has written them as real as the reader is, and that is what makes the novel so easily read."

The Scrotum Toad

Tangle is a tree-hugger who is often mistaken for a glamorous witch. She is proud of her organic smallholding in the heart of Africa.

When threatened by a bullying and corrupt businessman who starts trashing the environment and the local people, who can she turn to?

Surely not that foul-mouthed Aussie TV presenter, nor those famous and fabulously wealthy international holidaymakers who suddenly invade her precious patch. And how could an international food-eating competition, sponsored by the USA's tin-eared goodwill ambassador, solve her problems?

Surrounded by xenophobic bickering, Tangle struggles to assert her authority, aided by some unlikely admirers.

The Scrotum Toad is an outrageous comic novel which will have the easily offended spluttering over their lattes. Nationalities, cultures and occupations are satirised shamelessly.

You have been warned.

Chill with a Book Reader Award Winner

"This is sooo funny. It was full of stereotypes and definitely not meant to be realistic and yet there were so many well observed truths about people and their preconceptions. I was a teacher and there are people like Jake in every school - cussed awkward. As for the rest, I certainly recognised them in my travels to USA and around UK. Wonderful book, made me laugh for days."

"I think anyone who reads this book would relate to the topics and to how the extreme has become the norm for many. It is not real or is it? I think readers can see someone in this book they could relate to."

Amazon review

"This is the equivalent of going to a comedian's gig and laughing for an hour. If you are very PC and can't abide humour that pokes fun at stereotypes you might not like it. But in many ways, his humour reminded me of Ben Elton. Outrageous and over the top, but never boring and often on the nail. I'm both an American and a Brit, dual passport holder, and the author has a field day putting two objectionable people from either side of the pond into an African holiday spot. It was hysterical. I laughed out loud and continued laughing even after I'd gone to make the dinner! A wonderful antidote to depression. Cheaper than tickets at the Comedy Night spot and well worth the read."

The Corncrake

Life is becoming precarious for an Anglo-German family living in England on the eve of the First World War. They have very different ideas about what they should do. And two of them don't know about a dangerous family secret.

A priestly father who promotes the duty of fighting for God, King and Country. A mother who flaunts her German heritage. A son full of Nietzsche, atheism and rebelliousness. What influence can each have over the talented daughter of the family, who has ideas of her own?

Irresponsible newspapers inventing stories of German atrocities and espionage stir up hatred against the family. Will pride and their strong personalities allow them to compromise and survive?

The Corncrake is a historical novel set in 1909-10

and 1914-15. It brings to life little-known facts about ordeals experienced far from the Front Line.

Chill with a Book Premier Award Winner

"The revving-up of hatred and ignorance was a unique and interesting way to present the war – with the media and the Church paving the way."

"Beautifully written with an engaging cast of characters. I found this both enlightening and disturbing."

"The discussion of the anti-German sentiments in Britain during the war and the movement for repatriation etc. was very good and eye-opening to anyone not well versed on the home front during World War I."

"Very impressive writing with an intellectual and educated edge. The more I ponder this book, the more I admire what it took to write it."

....

All These Novels Available on Amazon in Paperback and Kindle

—— \\\/// ——

Printed in Great Britain
by Amazon

38073471R00138